The Masters Review

ten stories

The Masters Review

The Masters Review Volume XI
Stories Selected by Peter Ho Davies
Edited by Cole Meyer, Brandon Williams, and Jen Dupree

Front cover design by Emelie Mano
Interior design by Kim Winternheimer and Julianne Johnson

ISBN: 978-1-7363695-6-2

Printed in the USA

To receive new fiction, contest deadlines,
and other curated content right to your inbox,
send an email to newsletter@mastersreview.com

The Masters Review

ten stories

Volume XI

Fredrick Kunkle • Patricia García Luján

Ikechukwu Roy Udeh-Ubaka • Tim Griffith

Danielle Claro • Clemintine Guirado

David DeGusta • Kathleen Latham

Sophia Zaklikowski • Jenna Abrams

Stories Selected by
Peter Ho Davies

Contents

Introduction

I'm a reluctant judge of literary competitions. Partly that's for practical reasons. As a slow reader it's a challenge to take on extra pages during a busy teaching semester, and impossible during MFA application season when I'm already encountering hundreds of manuscripts. I often find myself regretfully declining such invitations—it *is* an honor to be asked, after all—sometimes politely saying, *if only I was on sabbatical*, except when a sabbatical comes around it's still hard to say "yes" to the reading, especially for book prizes, when I'm supposed to be writing one of my own.

I feel guilty about this—serving as a judge is a generous act of literary citizenship—which is why occasionally, if the timing is just right, I take on one of these assignments. (In the case of this assignment for *The Masters Review*, they were nice/dogged enough to ask twice).

But I suspect my reluctance to judge runs deeper than the practical impediments. There are the usual the lofty philosophical reservations about the incommensurability of art, of course, but also the more anxious writerly neuroses. The doubt that I, and any writer, feels when judging our own work (how and when do we know it's any good?) inevitably spills over into the judging of others.

To judge, after all, is to *be* judged—for our choices, our taste—and none of us are quite so sure of that as we might wish (as betrayed by how vociferously we argue for or against the lastest Pulitzer, National Book Award, or Oscar winner; how affronted we are when something we hate wins; how diminished we feel when we don't "get" why something was picked).

Such doubts feel like weakness, and maybe they are, but they seem like the kind of "weakness" that may be essential to strong fiction, a space where writer (and reader) are often productively confronted by uncertainty and ambiguity—more doubt. Novels and stories, we might say, play out doubt—"things in doubt" would be a pretty good catch-all description of most drama, after all. Beyond this I've a sneaking sense that fiction—mine at least, and the fiction I cherish—is somehow antithetical to judgement. Judgement feels distant, from on high, *ex cathedra*. To read, to write, to empathize—these things feel close-up, intimate, entangled. On the page I'm not interested in good guys and bad guys, so much as in people who are both good and bad, which is to say "human," which is in turn reflected in my resistance to categorizing the pages these humans appear in as good or bad.

This may all seem very deflective, even disowning, perhaps especially to the writers and their work collected here, which would be a disservice. Part of the joy in being chosen, after all, is that someone dispels our own writerly doubt, replaces our judgement with their own. I've felt that relief myself. And yet, it's probably at the heart of my reluctance to judge—this whiff of usurpation. I spend some time in my recent book *The Art of Revision: The Last Word* thinking about what it means to finish our work, to arrive at doneness, the final draft. That's a distant, hard-won destination, but on rare, blessed occasions we know it when we get there, a recognition that strikes with the force of revelation. It's the point, I argue, at which we finally understand our own work, when we become the best *reader* of our own work, which is to say the best judge. And one way to know a story has arrived at that point of doneness is that we no longer care quite so much about the judgement of others. There's a conviction to the work, an essentialness. And paradoxically, perhaps *that's* the quality I responded to in each of these works: their conviction, the sense of their knowing themselves, the feeling that—contrary to the circumstances in which I encountered them—they weren't asking for and didn't require my judgement, just my reading.

—*Peter Ho Davies*
Guest Judge

The Dog

Fredrick Kunkle

L uther Jacobs ripped the blanket off, bolted out of bed and dressed in a hurry. His wife opened one eye as he jammed his foot down the leg of his blue jeans.

"What are you doing?" she asked.

"I'm going to talk to that man."

"It's Sunday morning."

"Exactly."

Celeste squinted at the radio clock.

"Really?" she asked in a sleepy voice. "I can't even hear him."

"I can."

She propped herself on an elbow and turned to the window. Luther stood, also listening. Then it started, the fierce low barking of their neighbor's dog. Like a distant drumbeat pulsing through the thin walls and wooden floorboards of their bedroom, just at the edge of their perception, just loud enough that it touched Luther's last nerve.

"Now you hear it?"

"Barely. Put some cotton in your ears and come back to bed."

On the nightstand lay a plastic bag of cotton balls she had purchased for just this reason.

"No way. I'm done with this bullshit," Luther said. "This ain't about the dog anymore."

"What are you going to do?"

"Talk to him."

"Just call the police."

"Uh, uh. We'll talk first. Neighbor to neighbor, man to man."

"I don't know, baby. I think he's a little crazy."

"So am I right now. So. Am. I."

Luther buttoned his shirt and stalked out. He paused at the top of the stairs, peering through the window blinds at his neighbor's property. More snow had fallen overnight. It smoothed the edges of things, transforming the coal-blackened streets and homes into a picturesque scene of almost photographic contrast.

His neighbor's yard, encircled by a four-foot-high chainlink fence, contained an aluminum tool shed, a wood pile, a steel barrel for burning trash and several doghouses assembled from scraps of lumber. Only one doghouse was occupied. A massive German shepherd, its shaggy winter coat yellowish and black against the snow, moved in predatory circles at the limit of its chain. The dog seemed to glide over the snow, sometimes hurling itself at some unseen torment, until the chain tightened and yanked it back.

Luther let the blinds fall. The sight of the dog angered him but also made him wary and less certain about going next door, not so much because of the dog but because of what it said about its owner. His neighbor wasn't the only jackass in town with a nasty dog or a Confederate flag or a gun rack in his pickup, though this dude had it all. On the other hand, Luther had lived in the town long enough to know that lots of these characters only looked mean. This guy appeared to be a Steelers fan, judging from his bumper stickers, and might be a mechanic like Luther, too.

But Luther was no fool. Folks here, oh-so-smiley-faced and welcoming on the surface, often hid these twisted and bitter small-town souls. Everybody, even the mild Sunday school types, seemed always a little suspicious of everybody else: newcomers, outsiders, their own kids, the government. The longer you knew them, the more likely that the suspicion and ugliness seeped out, especially when it came to Black folks like him. Luther often pretended not to hear or see it, instead filing it away. He didn't want a fight, that's for sure. He would knock at the door, he would be polite. He would stay calm, no matter what. His father always said ninety-nine percent of all people are good people.

Luther stepped outside, still buttoning his quilted wool coat, and damn. The cold bit like fire. He moved slow, boots creaking over icy porch steps, and onto the sidewalk where everything—the ordered, clapboard houses with their tiny yards and low wooden porches—looked like a clone of everything else. Even the 4x4s, shoehorned into narrow driveways and caked with road salt and coal dust, looked alike, including Luther's. Almost every single house was in need of paint or repair, his neighbor's most of all. Its sagging chainlink fence gaped with holes that had been more or less stitched together with twisted coat hangers; an upper window had been patched with duct tape; the front downspout swung loose. There was a quality about the place not just of poverty but of recklessness, and Luther wondered whether he had been just as reckless, just as impulsive, to settle here. His older brother, who had driven the U-Haul and helped him find work before shipping out for an Army base in Frankfurt, said the area was part of Appalachia, as if that explained everything.

Luther ignored the NO TRESPASSING sign and, more jittery than he expected, stepped onto his neighbor's porch. A handwritten sign said: *Door Bell broke. KNOCK.* Luther rapped with his knuckles, too lightly, and rapped again, louder. The dog out back began to bark, but no one stirred. Icy snow skittered like sequins over the porch floor, piling up near a motorcycle covered with a plastic tarp. It was a motocross bike whose back wheel was missing, its twin forks propped on a greasy block of wood.

Luther bent close to a window—inconspicuously, having been taught it was rude to peek inside a home from the front door—but all he could see were cardboard boxes stacked in the foyer. As he turned to go, a dark figure lunged at the window, like a huge fish rising from the bottom of a lake. Luther jumped back as the front door opened.

"What the hell?" the man said, with an odd note of amusement in his voice. He was wiry and short, with wavy brown hair that fell to his shoulders, Jesus-like, and a grin that looked too wide for his narrow face.

"Oh, hey—sorry to trouble you," Luther said, and introduced himself by name. "I live next door."

"I know where you live."

His neighbor grinned harder, as if the two of them were sharing some inside joke. His large square teeth were very shiny and curved inward.

"I thought it best to stop by in person," Luther said. "I didn't mean to wake you…"

"Little late for that now."

"I'm sorry. I can come back later."

"Never mind. Something eating at ya?" The neighbor tucked his thumbs under his wide leather belt and planted two bare feet on the porch, as if to show he could stand there all day if need be. His belt buckle, engraved with *Lucky 13* and a skull, was as big as the back of his hand, which displayed some sort of faded, homemade tattoo. "Must be something brought you over here," the man said, and grinned harder.

Those teeth, Luther thought. And then he spotted the butt of a gun tucked into the man's belt, far back on his hip. Or a knife. Maybe a cellphone.

Luther's heart skipped, and a cold tremor snaked up his back. He tried to remember why this visit had seemed so urgent and likely to succeed, but the only thought in his head was how bad it was going, how his attempt at diplomacy was already playing out in ways he had not predicted.

"Well," Luther said, "I came by to ask if maybe there wasn't a way to keep your dog from barking?"

"My dog?"

"Yes. He barks all the time. Day and night, actually. Is it possible you could maybe take him inside, at least when people are sleeping?"

"You come about the dog? Zorro?"

"Well, our bedroom window is right up there, over the yard, and we…"

"Ohhhhhh," the man said, and he stepped farther onto the porch, slapping each foot down. He rested his hands on his hips in a theatrical way that concealed whatever it was he was carrying on his belt. "Is that where your bedroom is?"

"That's right."

"Well, imagine that. Because I was laying in mine about fifteen minutes ago and started wondering, *Now, where is that Negro's bedroom, I wonder? The bedroom where he sleeps with his Negro-loving wife? Maybe he'll drop by today to let me know.*"

There it was: almost exactly what Luther had expected, what he expected from almost any white man, what seemed to be always on their lips even when saying nothing at all. Yet, no matter how many times it happened before or would happen again, the words hit with such force that Luther recoiled, even flinched a little. He balled both fists inside his coat pockets, as his heart kicked out spurts of adrenaline. Yet, he also felt a quiver of doubt, wondering whether he had heard what he just heard, whether what had just happened, happened. A look of mock sympathy appeared on the man's face.

"I'm sorry," he said. "I just realized what's going on here. You can't read. I mean, I put a sign down there, posted right on the front gate in plain English, that says *No Trespassing*. Which, if you could read, you would know that's what you're doing. Ain't that so?"

His neighbor crinkled up his eyes with some private mirth, even as the lower part of his face became stony, almost hateful. He flicked his fingers, as if to whisk Luther away.

Luther, almost without thinking, removed first one hand from his coat pocket and then the other. His last fight, in the Marines, had lasted only a few minutes—an explosion of pent-up, almost joyful rage that would become the source of long-enduring regret almost from the moment he drove his fist into the bones of the other man's face.

"Sir, I did not come here to quarrel," Luther said, struggling to keep his teeth from chattering. "I did not come here to be insulted, either. I came because your dog woke us up this morning, and it wasn't the first time."

"Your wife is white, isn't she?" The man chuckled. "She's maybe whiter than me, I think. As I like to say, though, to each his own. Now, just the same, I'd appreciate if you would kindly get your Black ass off my porch. Because, like I said, you're a trespasser here. Otherwise, I'll call the cops."

"I'm leaving," Luther said. "But you need to do something about that dog."

Luther was about to say more. Instead, he dug his fists into his coat and went sideways down the steps, careful to keep his eyes on the man. When he passed the front gate, he shoved it closed with his boot.

"Hey!" the man yelled. "You break my gate, you'll pay for it!"

Celeste was inside making breakfast and listening to *Car Talk* when Luther entered the kitchen. The room, steamy with the smell of coffee and bacon, seemed smaller than usual. Celeste, turning the bacon strips with a fork, cracked up at something as Luther dropped onto a chair and, trembling with fury, unbuttoned his coat.

"Hey! You with the boots!" Celeste said, as if this exaggerated display of outrage were part of the radio show. "You're tracking snow all over the place."

Bright puddles had already formed around his feet.

"So I'm guessing your little chat next door didn't go so well?" she said. "What happened?"

Luther, still thinking over what he should have said or done and how intentions seldom if ever go the way one plans, twirled a coat button with his fingertips.

"Hello? Luther? Cat got your tongue? What happened?"

"We almost got into it, that's what. Right there on the porch."

Celeste let her arms drop to her side, exasperated. "What did you say to him, Lu?"

"Me?"

"Yes, you. You left here spitting fire."

"I didn't say shit, Celeste. I hardly said anything and the guy attacked me."

"He hit you?"

"No, but might as well have."

"Were you polite?"

"Yes, I was goddamn polite. And he's a goddamn racist."

Celeste laid the spatula on the counter. She turned off the radio. "I'm so sorry, Luther."

"It had to happen, you know."

"I'm so, so sorry."

"It's just this place. It's the neighborhood. It's the whole goddamn town."

Tears welled in her eyes, and she turned back to the skillet.

"Besides which, he met me at the door with a gun."

"A gun?"

"Yes. I mean, I think so."

"Luther, you need to call the cops."

"But I'm not even sure. It could have been a knife or something. It's not like he actually threatened me with it."

"You should call the cops anyway, put him on record."

"Oh, sure. That'll make him a friend for life," he said.

Luther spent the rest of the day replaying in his mind everything that had happened on his neighbor's porch. A light snow fell that afternoon and into the night, and when the alarm went off the next morning, he went out to shovel snow before work. The shovel was bent, which made the job frustrating, but at least the dog wasn't out. He hadn't heard it, either, since the previous morning. Maybe the friendly neighborhood Klansman, for all his bravado, had decided to deal with his dog after all.

Luther had just started dusting the pickup's windshield with a broom when its bristles hit something half buried in snow. It was a package of Oreos—and he knew right away how it had gotten there, and why, before unfolding the note.

LOVE ME SOME OREOS!!! it said.

Luther crumpled the paper. He reached for the package but pulled his hand back, thinking it might be boobytrapped, maybe coated in dog shit, and instead used the broom to shove it onto the ground. He examined the cellophane wrapper, which was clean and intact, before ripping it open and shaking the contents through the fence into his neighbor's yard. Then he crumpled the wrapper and tossed that over, too.

Suddenly, the German shepherd appeared, off its chain and bolting straight for Luther. It sprang at the fence with such force Luther thought the animal might knock it down. He gripped the broom like a baseball bat, as the dog leaped almost high enough to clear the fence. An upper window scraped open. His neighbor— naked to the waist, damp hair slicked behind each ear—leaned out, white knuckles gripping the windowsill.

"Hey! What do you think you're doing throwing that shit in my yard?"

Luther gave him the finger. But the neighbor had already turned his attention to the dog, which was wolfing down cookies scattered across the snow.

"Zorro!" he yelled. "Get the hell out of that!"

Luther, still clutching the broom, stormed inside. He found Celeste upstairs, making the bed.

"What happened?"

"I'm calling the cops."

"On our neighbor?"

"Yes, him. The asshole put Oreos on my truck."

Celeste, making a puzzled face, went to the window. The dog was chained now, trotting in circles.

"Probably has a sugar high," Luther said.

"What on earth are you talking about?"

"The dog. Look at him."

"Luther, I have no idea what's going on."

"Our friend left Oreos on my truck. *OR-EE-Os.* Get it?"

"I don't see anything. I just see the dog."

Luther, cradling the telephone receiver under his chin, punched at the numbers and paced.

"I dumped them in his goddamn yard. I should have poisoned them first."

Luther banged down the receiver, wrong number.

"Calm down."

"I am calm. I'm very, very calm."

"What are you going to say?"

"What do you mean, *What am I going to say?*"

"What are you going to tell the police? *My neighbor left some cookies in my yard?*"

"The man put Oreos on my truck, which is harassment. It's harassment and trespassing and no different than burning a goddamn cross."

"Lu."

Luther waved his hand.

"Hello: this is Luther Jacobs," he said. "I'd like to file a complaint."

For the next few days, Luther and Celeste waited and sometimes worried that calling the borough police could escalate things. Then they wondered whether the police had done anything at all. There was no follow-up, no nothing, which made Luther think his complaint had been shit-canned or even laughed off. On the other hand, weeks passed without any obvious provocations from his neighbor.

Little things happened, though. Ambiguous things that suggested someone was messing with them. Celeste's car tire went flat twice in two weeks, but they couldn't find a leak. Then Luther's pickup was keyed—a deep gash, running fender to fender. Luther, knowing from years of working in body shops that vandals sometimes keyed vehicles at random in parking lots, couldn't be sure where or when the damage occurred. He retouched the paint and became more careful about where he parked.

Always in the background was the dog, this stupid, annoying, vicious dog with its incessant barking, and the stupid, shrunken man who kept him. Through spring and early summer as the weather changed, Luther felt almost trapped in his own house. He disliked opening windows or walking around his yard or even sitting outside because of the dog, which often flew at the fence in a spitting rage when Luther was near. Even worse, the dog and its owner crowded into Luther's thoughts no matter what Luther was doing. He might be driving to the grocery store or to work or be in the middle of buffing out a coat of paint when some flash of memory would intrude, some glimpse of that morning on the porch or dialing the police or some other ridiculous and insulting moment that yanked him away and into the past, leaving him in a state of agitation almost as violent as when the actual event occurred. The more these memories reappeared, the deeper they burned. It required effort to shift focus, to dispel the interruption and quiet the rage that seemed always to be bubbling near the surface. Celeste said he was depressed, he should see someone. Whatever.

It became so bad that the sound of a dog or the sight of a dog sometimes startled him, and he began to dislike all dogs. It seemed almost crazy to him, the way this sudden hatred would pour forth in a scalding rush. It was as if he had some black gunk churning and oozing inside of him, and his inability to not so much forget about everything but put things in their place and move on seemed more and more like a personal affliction. How had a dumb beast gained such power over him? Had he, Luther, changed? Or had things changed around him? Like all fixations, this one complicated his life and made it seem smaller, too, until the thought entered his head of killing the damn thing—poisoning, shooting, even clubbing it to death—and the very vividness of this new malice shocked and ashamed him still more.

Celeste brought home a parakeet that one of her co-workers at the Mini-Mart couldn't keep anymore. That distracted him for a while, though the jittery little creature shivered in a corner of its cage more than it ever sang. Luther also tried helping Celeste restore antique furniture, a hobby of hers that held out promise as a possible business, until he discovered that he had no patience for caning chairs and the like. And they planted a garden together—her half with flowers, his with vegetables—that took him several times to a dairy farm outside town to pick up free topsoil and cow manure.

On his way back one afternoon, Luther noticed how his neighbor had been working in his yard, too. The weeds at the bottom of the chainlink fence had been uprooted, and in their place were several shiny green flagstones. Then—peering closer—Luther saw with slow-dawning amazement that these flagstones were watermelons laid end to end like a string of beads. Each was scrawled with a black letter that, taken all together, spelled *HOWDY!*

Luther slammed the truck into park. He flung open its door and stalked across the yard for the wheelbarrow before realizing he had left the engine running. He pushed the wheelbarrow under the tailgate, leaped into the truck bed and snatched at the shovel, thinking that if he had an axe, he would climb his neighbor's fence and smash every single watermelon to bits. Dirt flew as he shoveled the wheelbarrow full and jumped down, gripping its handles and driving it crazily toward the garden. He dumped one load, then stormed inside.

Celeste was at the kitchen table. Their eyes met a moment before she buried her face in her arms. Luther sat beside her, removed a work glove and laid his hand on her shoulder. Then he got up, almost choking with rage and the instantaneous and odd realization that, for reasons he couldn't understand, some part of his anger was directed at her.

"We should just move, Luther."

"That's exactly what that little piece of shit wants."

"He's not just hateful. He's dangerous. He's gone out of his way to torment us. I'm frightened, and you must be, too."

"I'm not frightened. I'm pissed."

"Sometimes it's the same thing."

Luther snorted and headed back outside. He worked the topsoil and manure into the garden until exertion consumed most of his rage. Maybe she was right. Maybe they should find someplace where no one would bother them. Someplace like the farm he visited, with its ancient barn and Dutch hex signs, its air pungent and earthy, its herd of dairy cows scattered like a black-and-white jigsaw puzzle over a hillside. It was beautiful, quiet, green. The few words the farmer had spoken sounded foreign, though—and that's what it was, a place that, for all its beauty, was utterly foreign to Luther, inexplicable and forbidding.

Luther started to sweep up around the truck when his neighbor's dog shot toward him out of nowhere, off its chain and flying so fast it looked as if it might leap the fence. Then came another—a Doberman pinscher that was younger and smaller than the first, its finely muscled limbs sleek with speed. Both animals threw themselves at the rickety fence, hitting it with their front paws until the whole thing rattled and shook, all the while barking and snarling as the silhouette of his neighbor passed like a silent ghost behind an upstairs window.

Luther, half backing up, went inside. Celeste was upstairs, wallpapering the bathroom.

"Our friend has a new dog," Luther said. "Did you see it?"

"You're joking."

"Both vicious, both running around crazy."

"Loose?"

"Yes—in his yard. Two now."

"He's crazy, Luther."

The next day during lunch break, Luther drove to the State Police barracks in Punxsutawney. He waited in an anteroom stocked with *Good Housekeeping, Field & Stream*, and several hot rod magazines, shivering from the air-conditioning. The place began to feel like a meat locker before Vernon's face appeared with a grin in the bulletproof window of the armored door.

"Took you long enough," Luther said, following him inside.

"We don't usually let in bad actors like you," Vernon said.

"Yeah, right."

They kidded and talked as Vernon tapped at a console that had been around since the dawn of the Computer Age. Slowly, laboriously, a printout emerged.

"That's your boy," Vernon said. Luther squinted at the block of text:

NAME: Paul Michael Goddard
DOB: 4/21/52
ADDRESS: 1122 Philadelphia Street, Arcadia, Pa.
HEIGHT: 5'9" // **WEIGHT:** 175 lbs // **EYES:** Brown
// **HAIR:** Brown
RACE: Caucasian **ALIASES:** "Poncho" "Scorch"
TATTOOS//DISTINGUISHING FEATURES: Upper left
chest (cobra)//Right bicep (mermaid)//Left hand
(rune)//Abdomen (~4" vertical scar)

SUPERIOR COURT, JUNIATA COUNTY
Count 1: Felon poss. handgun — GUILTY: Two years,
Six months
Count 2: Aggravated Assault — GUILTY: 18 months,
c/c Count #1
Count 3: Poss. CDS, 2nd degree — GUILTY: 18
months, c/c Count #1

SUPERIOR COURT, JUNIATA COUNTY
Count 1: Auto Theft/Operate Chop-Shop - GUILTY:
18 months
Count 2: Witness Intimidation — NOLO: 18 months,
c/c Count #1
Count 3: Resisting/Assault on LEO — GUILTY: 12
months, c/c Count #1

SUPERIOR COURT, JEFFERSON COUNTY
Count 1: Assault — NOT GUILTY, Dismissed
Count 2: Animal Cruelty — NOT GUILTY, Dismissed
Count 3: Threats - NOT GUILTY, Dismissed
Count 4: Bad Checks - GUILTY: Three months
probation

"Can't say I'm surprised," Luther said.

"Me neither. Of course, I've seen lots worse," Vernon said. He forced a chuckle, but his eyes appeared sad, maybe resigned, behind their sheen of professional coolness.

It was an odd coincidence that two military brats who started out in Detroit should reconnect in western Pennsylvania. When Luther and Vernon had attended high school, people who saw Vernon on stage or heard his voice predicted a big future with Motown or some other label. He was handsome, loose, a little cocky, fun to be around. Over the years he became more reserved, circumspect, maybe because of his time in the military or law enforcement or being the first Black trooper in these parts. Vernon often complained that, despite testing near the top of the promotion lists, he hadn't advanced in rank, but at least his co-workers no longer hazed him. But Luther hadn't seen Vernon since Vernon and his wife, Bonnie, moved to the mountains northeast of there.

"They ever find the asshole who put the noose in your locker?" Luther whispered.

"You kidding?" Vernon said, adjusting a framed picture of his wife, who was also Black.

"Figures. How can you even trust any of these dudes?"

"Who said I do?" Vernon said. "I don't trust nobody. Not even you. Maybe not even me."

They laughed. Another trooper, rising from a desk with a sheaf of papers in his fist, shot them a quizzical glance.

"So what's my move here, seeing as the borough police haven't done shit?" Luther asked.

"Not much you can do, is there? About a bag of cookies?"

"That's exactly what Celeste said."

"Seems to me you ought to build a bigger fence or buy a bigger dog."

"Or a gun."

"Always an option," Vernon said, chuckling. "If there's one thing rednecks understand, it's guns."

Vernon walked Luther to the parking lot to show off his new toy, a black Harley Road King with fat pipes and a massive chrome headlight. Luther climbed on and fired it up, whistling at the motor's throaty rumble and quick-building heat.

"Maybe some day," Luther shouted, though privately he was glad that Celeste would never let him buy a motorcycle. He hit the kill switch, handed back the keys and showed Vernon where his pickup truck had been scratched before climbing in to go.

"Hey," Vernon said, through the open window. "You know I'm kidding about the gun, right?"

"How so?"

"It'll get you into lots more trouble than it ever gets you out of."

"And yet what's that right there?" Luther said, pointing to Vernon's service weapon.

"That's different."

"Uh-huh."

When Luther arrived home, both dogs were roaming free next door. Celeste was in the kitchen in her Mini-Mart outfit.

"How's our new friend?" Luther asked.

"Kind of cute, to be honest."

"Cute?"

"He sorta looks like a little fudge brownie."

"Like a fudge brownie with teeth."

The next morning, Luther found Celeste in the kitchen again, though bleary and wired out from her overnight shift. She sat at the kitchen table with a box of miniature chocolate donuts, thumbing through an antiques magazine. Luther poured a cup of coffee and joined her, lacing his work boots as she told how some drunken fool had driven off and ripped a hose out of a gas pump. The Mini-Mart's manager, a kid half her age, didn't know where to find the emergency shut-off until she showed him. And then the manager got pissed because she left the till open during the commotion, though both counted the receipts twice and not a nickel was missing.

Luther listened and made wisecracks about life at the Mini-Mart. But he also felt bad, knowing how Celeste's job, especially night shifts and weekends, exposed her to risks. There were sometimes fights, and it had been robbed at gunpoint at least twice, yet they wouldn't have been able to make ends meet without her paycheck. Luther grabbed his lunch bag and bent to kiss her hair.

"You know your name patch is coming off, right?" she said.

"Yeah, it's been like that a while. It's okay."

"Let me fix it for you. It'll take a second."

Celeste pulled down an old candy tin she used as a sewing box and went to work. Her hair smelled like lemon shampoo and cigarette smoke and her breath felt cool against his chest as the needle darted in and out. If not for work, he would have slipped his hands around her cowgirl hips and led her back upstairs.

"Hey!" Luther said. "You jabbed me!"

"Stand still," she said, "and you won't get stuck."

"I am standing still. It's bleeding."

"You're not bleeding, you big baby. There. It's done."

She gave him a playful shove toward the door. Sunshine was skimming over the dew as Luther unlocked the pickup when, suddenly, both dogs came tearing around the corner of his neighbor's house. They ran shoulder to shoulder, hurling themselves at the fence with a ferocity that seemed more violent than before, as if each dog had driven the other into a state of frenzy that also aroused something instinctual in Luther, some ancient, captivating terror of the pack.

"Zorro!" his neighbor screamed from the back of the house. "Zorro! Goddamnit, get in here!"

The German shepherd broke off, trotting toward his master's voice. But the young Doberman wouldn't quit. It kept lunging and barking until his neighbor appeared, barefoot and shirtless, still screaming and cursing. He was all bones, maybe high or maybe drunk, and hurried across the yard with a heavy black skillet in his hand. If anything, the dog became more crazed the closer the man got.

"Nigger!" he screamed. "Goddamnit, I'm talking to you!"

Shock, then realization washed over Luther as his neighbor repeated the slur several times: It was not just one of the most hateful things anyone could utter, a word that led to the most unspeakable violence, a word people had been killed over. All at once it also became clear from the man's intonation that this was his animal's name. He bore down on the dog, wielding the iron skillet like a club.

"Goddamn your soul!" Goddard shrieked, and swung the skillet at the dog's head. He missed, slipped on the wet grass, got up, and swung again, this time hitting the dog's rump. The dog, hunched and squealing in pain, scurried off. Goddard, who seemed not to have even seen Luther there, chased after it, muttering profanities.

That evening, Luther bought a gun. He had debated all day at work, obsessing to the point that he singed the paint on a Mustang with the electric buffer, and didn't make a final decision until driving home. He went past Duncan's Guns & Ammo—glancing at its elaborate rooftop display with a plastic horse and an actual stagecoach—before doubling back into the parking lot. Customers milled by the entrance and crowded the display cases inside. It was mostly men, and all but two of them, who looked Spanish, were white. On the wall hung a yellowing poster with pictures of Hitler, Stalin and Mao saying, "*Experts Agree…Gun Control Works!!!*"

The clerk seemed unusually happy to help, which was good because there was a bewildering variety of handguns. Luther settled on a used .357-caliber Colt Python and counted out $266 in cash while the clerk handled the paperwork. Once Luther was alone in the pickup, he opened the polished wooden case to have another look and felt the uncanny thrill of a firearm in his hands, as if the steel itself were invested with power.

Weeks passed without his mentioning the gun to Celeste. The secrecy, which he believed inconsequential at first, gathered a weight of its own that felt strange and unsettling. It occurred to him more than once to return the revolver or, because that seemed somehow embarrassing, get rid of it some other way.

Then Luther awoke one night to a loud disturbance outside. The neighbor's dogs were barking, and it sounded as if a garbage can filled with broken glass had crashed to the ground. Celeste, asleep with cotton balls in her ears, snored beside him, oblivious. He lay awake for a time as wind howled through the leaky windows, letting his eyes adjust to the twilight and trying to sift through the noises for signs of danger. He rose and crept to the window. The full moon scattered crooked shadows on the ground. Then came more banging, more barking, and another crash as if someone was breaking in.

Luther went to the chair where he often tossed his clothes, scooped an armful, and stepped into the hall to dress, so as not to wake Celeste. He returned just as quietly to the closet and felt along the highest shelf, beyond Celeste's reach, where he had hidden the gun. He crept down the stairs, holding the revolver stiff-armed in front of him.

Outside, the sky was thick with stars—blue, white, even pink—scattered like seeds over a blackened field. Leaves scuttled across the driveway as he sneaked down the back steps, feeling tense and absurd for what would almost certainly be a false alarm. Yet, his heart slammed at his chest as if he were the one trespassing.

Then something stirred, something close by in the bushes near the kitchen window. Almost simultaneously, two eyes blinked in his neighbor's yard—animal eyes, reflective, unmoving, greenish blue. They seemed locked on him, appraising, hunting; the longer he looked, the brighter they burned. Luther raised the revolver and tightened his grip, seized by the sudden, irrational fear he might drop it.

How many times had Luther imagined this moment, even before he purchased the gun? How many times had he aligned the gunsights between an imaginary pair of eyes, envisioned the muzzle flash, felt its kick, heard the sharp concussive roar rippling through empty streets? Then several fat and stupid borough cops pounding on his door, perhaps with his redneck neighbor in tow. Luther would admit nothing, maybe say nothing at all, except: "Prove it."

Across the driveway, the pair of eyes blinked again. A chain rattled as it dragged, link by link by link, over the floor of a dogbox, gathering speed. The moment the animal sprang—reaching the fence before the second dog had bolted from its box, too—Luther dropped the revolver. Then something exploded behind him, another commotion in the bushes below the kitchen window that was not a burglar or Goddard but a raccoon—no, a stray cat!—that streaked across the dark yard.

Other dogs in the neighborhood began to bark as Luther knelt, almost panicky, patting the damp grass for the revolver. A light blinked on in an upper room of Goddard's house, transforming the dark taped-up window into a yellow square brighter than the moon.

Luther found the gun. He wrapped his trembling fingers around it. He pointed it first at the dogs, then at the house, then at the illuminated window, his finger curled on the trigger. His eyes watered as the gunsights swam in and out of the window until at last the silhouette of a man appeared, his giant head topped with a wild nimbus of hair and his torso's crazily distorted shadow thrown onto the wall behind him.

Luther, as if stung, yanked the gun away. Then he knelt, gripping onto a shock of damp grass to keep from falling, gasping for breath while it seemed that every dog for miles and miles around was barking and howling.

FREDRICK KUNKLE *is a journalist and writer based in Washington DC.*

Bad Guys

Patricia García Luján

I

When I pick her up from school, she climbs onto the booster and pulls her seatbelt into the lock. I squeeze her knee and ask about her day. She tells me they ate mac and cheese for lunch. She says there was a safety drill in the afternoon.

There are no earthquakes where we live. Our constant source of anxiety comes from the ocean instead. Super storms that build off its warming waters. I always joke that hurricanes are the most considerate of all natural disasters. At least they give us a week's warning, I say. More than enough time to evacuate, pack our valuables, board up our windows.

Do you mean a fire drill? I ask. A row of SUVs snakes in front of us.

No, fire drills are when we go outside, she says. During safety drills, we lock the doors and hide in the art closet. Can I have a mint?

I reach into my tote bag and pull out an Altoid from the tin. She likes how the menthol tickles her tongue. I ask her if they've ever done these kinds of drills before. She's in kindergarten and it seems too early, too premature for a girl her age.

A few times, she says and cracks the mint with her teeth. But I never like them because it's always super dark in the closet and we have to be super quiet.

She tells me they stand there in silence. The teacher holds an index finger over her lips the whole time. All she ever hears are her classmates' breaths going in and out, in and out.

My hands start to get clammy. I turn on the radio and change the subject. I don't want to press any more. I worry about leading her mind to places I don't think it's ready to go.

A security guard waves us goodbye as our car leaves the school. I notice the gun stored inside the holster of his belt. It hangs there, thick and matte black. I wonder whether my daughter notices it in the mornings as she walks into her classroom. If she sees it sitting there in the man's belt, right around the same height as her small head.

When we get home, I email the principal and start off with a polite greeting before admonishing her on whether this is necessary. Aren't they a little too young for this? I write. What do you even tell the kids they're hiding from?

She replies in what I can tell is a standard response by now. The drills are required by state law. Teachers don't go into specifics with the younger students. And no, it's never too early. She reminds me of the name of an elementary school in Connecticut.

It's awful, she writes, but it's the world we live in.

I go against my better instinct and Google the incident. Reading about terrible things on the internet is my personal form of self-harm. I remember it took place when I was still in college, before I was married and had my daughter, before I worried about the height of a playground or counted the hours between fevers. The only life I had to worry about was my own.

As I skim through the Wikipedia page, I wince at some of the details on the screen. I'd forgotten how young the victims were. Sixes and sevens listed one after the other.

I'd forgotten how it happened only ten days before Christmas.

My therapist once suggested I try to channel my fears into something a little more productive. You're a writer, she said during one of our sessions, why not re-write some of those traumas? Banish them off with a happier ending.

I open a new document on my screen and continue to go down a school shooting rabbit hole, which I now justify as research. I fail to notice when my daughter walks into my office.

Mami, what's that? my daughter asks, breaking my trance. Is that a gun?

What? I say and slam the laptop shut. How do you know about guns?

Why are you looking at guns? she asks and fishes another orange goldfish from the bag in her hands.

That's nothing, that's just something I have to do for work.

You work with guns?

No, no, I don't, I say and struggle with how to continue, how to explain to her that I often sit in my office and ignore her for hours so I can write violent little stories about people that aren't real.

Chiqui, how do you know what a gun looks like?

She stands there barefoot; her toes twitch against the floor.

Lily's brother plays a video game where he chases after bad guys with guns.

Oh. I get up and together we walk back into the kitchen. And you play the game, too? I ask and make a mental note to call Lily's mother later.

No, we just watch him play and kill a bunch of bad guys.

Kill? I ask.

Yes, she says. That's what you do to bad guys. You kill them.

I look at her blue eyes and the freckles across her nose and try to ignore the fact that she's talking about murder. I find myself at a loss. We haven't even touched the subject of death yet. When her great-grandmother passed away, we only said she was gone. As lapsed Catholics, her father and I are against teaching her the concept of heaven and hell. But back then, she was only three. We didn't need to get into specifics.

Mami, have *you* ever seen a gun in real life? she asks while I open and close drawers, looking for nothing.

No, I lie to her. Never.

Later that night, I'm making dinner while she sits on the couch watching a cartoon about a talking Australian dog. Her hair is combed back and dripping wet. A damp circle forms in the back of her pajamas.

My husband is in the kitchen with me. I whisper to him about today's safety drill while he pours me a generous glass of white wine.

They make the whole class hide in the same supply closet, I say. They shove twenty kids in there.

It's fine, he says. He and I are wired differently. While I doomscroll and look up every weird symptom on WebMD, he plays chess on his phone, meditates in the garden in the morning.

It's not fine, I hush yell at him. They're traumatizing these poor kids.

My nervous system is already off. Adrenaline courses through my veins and my chest hurts. My fight-or-flight is activated once again.

Ceci, she probably doesn't even understand what's going on, he says. I wouldn't worry about it too much.

We both look at her as she sits in a contorted pose on the sofa and laughs to herself.

I just don't want her to grow up like I did, I say. Afraid all the time.

He tells me there's nothing to worry about and pulls me in for a hug. He can sense when I need help remembering how to breathe. Our chests touch and I can feel his rise up against mine and then retreat. I follow his lead and fall into a calming rhythm.

This isn't like that, he says. We live in a good neighborhood, Ceci. It's different here.

I look at our front door made of glass.

Yes, I say, you're right. I'll stop.

I notice that we'd left the door unlocked.

II

They rang the doorbell at around 10:30 on a Wednesday morning while Socorro was busy mopping up the kitchen. La India sang about heartbreak on the radio and the smell of purple disinfectant clung to the damp tile floor.

Ceci was upstairs, alone. She'd stayed home that day with a stomachache. Her mother, at work, had left her tucked inside her king-sized bed with *The Little Mermaid* on TV and a glass of medicinal Coca-Cola with ice on her nightstand. Her older brother was in school. Her father no longer lived in the house.

Hola, Socorro said, when she approached the door. Who's there?

She stared through the peephole. Outside, one of them covered the small glass dome with the palm of their hand.

Hola?

All the masked men stayed silent.

Socorro stepped away and the doorbell rang again.

Ceci heard it ring twice too and thought it was her aunt checking up on her. Her aunt often showed up at their house unannounced. Unlike her mother, she didn't have to go into an office every morning. She had the time.

Socorro approached the door again, thinking perhaps someone was playing a prank on her. Maybe the girl who worked in the house next door. The two of them weren't exactly friends, but they sometimes shared a cigarette on the street in between their lunch and dinner duties.

She looked through the peephole once more.

Who's there? she asked, and the masked men stood quietly. They didn't mind waiting.

Socorro pressed her ear to the thick wood. Later, when the police interrogate her, Socorro will swear she heard the girl from next door giggling softly on the other side. That's why I opened the door, she'll say. I never would've had I known who was there. But PoliCaracas won't believe her. Nor will Ceci's mother, who'll fire her the next morning. No one will.

Once the door was pushed open, Ceci heard voices she did not recognize. Low, masculine voices. And even before she ran to the top of the stairs and peered down, before she saw a hand clamped around Socorro's mouth and another pressing a small silver gun into the softness of her temple, Ceci knew those voices could only belong to bad men.

She, like all the kids around her, had known about bad men for much of her short life. The adults whispered about them when they thought the kids weren't listening. Parents swapped horror stories about them breaking into houses through the windows and stealing cars parked just outside on the street. For a week, they all talked about the father of one of the boys in her school that was shot for wearing a gold watch. They said that man was asking for trouble. The parents didn't think their sons and daughters noticed the barbed wire on the fences and the bars over the windows and the locks on top of the steering wheels. But children always know more than parents prefer to believe.

Ceci ran back to the room and stepped inside her father's walk-in closet, empty for almost a year. After their dad packed up his things and moved into a one-bedroom apartment on the other side of the Guaire with his lover, Ceci had fashioned the space into her own little playhouse. She'd hung blankets from the pants rack, folded doll clothes inside the drawers, plastered stickers all over the walls.

She slipped quietly into one of the closet's compartments and folded herself into the small rectangular space. She grabbed a blanket and draped it over her body. Beneath the fabric, Ceci could see nothing, but still she closed her eyes. She listened to her breath go in and out of her nose. Outside, Sebastian sang about the joys of living under the sea. On her mother's nightstand, the wireless telephone sat in its dock next to the watered-down glass of Coke. Ceci wondered if she could run fast enough to get it and come back. But she stayed there in the darkness, too afraid to try.

She wasn't sure how long she'd been hiding in there when she heard the low murmur of the closet door sliding open. Soft, measured footsteps touched the carpeted floor.

She felt someone hovering over her. She held her breath and wished herself invisible.

The blanket then started to slink away from her like falling sand. She froze and let it peel away until she sat there in her worn-down nightgown with dimpled cotton. Her hair was all over her face, her unicorn underwear slightly on display.

A man towered above.

When the police ask her later what he looked like, she won't remember much. Not the white scar on his forehead or his patchy beard, or his flaky, dry knuckles. The only thing she'll remember is his pink T-shirt. Pink was her favorite color and she thought it was odd for him to be wearing it because her mother always said pink was for girls.

The two looked at each other for a second.

Ven, he said and reached out his hand. Let's go.

Which one's your room? he asked outside in the hallway and the girl pointed at the door to their right.

Downstairs, she could hear the other bad men busy at work. There was the skid of furniture. Cables dragging against the floor. The opening and closing of drawers. Someone turned on the CD player and ramped up the volume to Guns N' Roses.

The man opened the door to her bedroom and gently ushered her in. His hand pressed below the back of her neck. Once inside, he turned around and closed the door.

Sit, he said, gesturing to her twin bed.

She obeyed, not only because she was the kind of kid to follow orders from adults, but because she'd noticed a black gun peeking out from his back pocket.

You don't go to school? the man asked. He stared at her and leaned his body against the door.

Ceci wondered if Socorro could hear her through the shut door if she screamed. She looked away and fixed her eyes on the dollhouse on the floor.

The man took a slow step closer to the bed.

She thought of her mother. She said she would call to check up on her, but the phone hadn't rung. She imagined her busy in her office, stamping papers, drinking cortaditos, all while this strange man stood inside of her room.

You don't speak? he asked.

I'm sick, she whispered. My stomach hurts.

Probably something you ate, he said and took another step closer.

Ceci remembered the raspado Socorro had gotten her yesterday afternoon after she finished her homework. She'd picked a red snow cone drenched with sticky condensed milk on the top. Her stomach turned when she thought of the strawberry-flavored ice sliding down her throat.

Where's Socorro? she asked. Her heartbeat raced.

The man gave her a weak smile and sat down. He rearranged his jeans and reached his hand behind his back. He placed something on the floor, but she couldn't see what because his torso was blocking her view.

She's in her room, he said. Don't worry about her, she's okay.

After they leave and Ceci finally feels brave enough to go down the stairs, she'll discover Socorro in her room, just as he said. She'll be tied up with bed sheets, her elbows bent in an unnatural position, her mouth stuffed with a pair of cotton socks. She'll be asleep, her face caked with dried blood, and she'll have an egg-sized bump over her left eyebrow, where one of the men smacked her with the blunt side of a revolver. Purple marks around her wrists won't go away for days.

Do you want to play a game? the man asked.

He leaned towards the dollhouse and pulled out a small stuffed unicorn. The girl hadn't seen that unicorn in weeks. She'd forgotten she'd stuck it in there.

What's her name? he asked.

Lili.

Hola Lili, yo soy Pito, he said in a high-pitched voice and laughed to himself.

Ceci somehow found herself laughing, too.

Shhh, the man said. Let's not talk too loud, okay? He pointed at the door again and tapped his lips with one of his index fingers.

Pito! a voice yelled from below. The man's expression sank. He shot up.

Here, he handed the stuffed animal to her.

Lie down behind your bed, he said.

He opened the door and peeked outside. He motioned her down with her hand. Before he left, he turned around and whispered. Don't come out, okay?

He walked out and made sure to leave the door slightly ajar, so that later, when the other men come upstairs, she'll hear Pito tell them where they can find her mother's jewelry, the make of her television, that there is no safe in either of the walk-in closets. She'll listen to him talk about her room—nothing there, only dolls, he'll say—and lead them into her brother's across the hall, where he'll tell them there's a steel baseball bat and some clothes—maybe you want some for your boy? he'll ask. They'll keep working for what seems like hours, even though it was less than one, and the door will stay as he left it, with only a sliver of light ever entering her room.

But for now, Ceci followed his instructions and laid down behind her bed. She held her unicorn in her arms and pressed her cheek to the wood. There, in the middle of the room, she saw his gun resting on the floor.

III

The first time I held a gun I was eight years old. Of course, I'd seen many before that. They were everywhere in La Cota, as common as our daily bread. I was in third grade, that's where it all started, in school, the place where we were supposed to go learn, but we only learned bad things. Things that should never be taught.

That day, la señorita Flores was teaching us about tildes, little sticks you add on top of certain letters on certain occasions. Señorita Flores was nice and patient. She would go over things we didn't understand, once, twice, three times, as long as we asked nicely. But most of us were hardly ever nice because being nice was for girls and for maricos. Instead, we mostly yelled at each other, calling the ones who asked questions idiotas even though we didn't know the answers either. We threw our notebooks and tumbled over chairs. We carved our initials in the wood and drew penises on the walls. We told dirty jokes, disgusting ones, and the girls would turn their heads and glare at us, but señorita Flores would laugh. She thought we were funny. She never got mad, even though everyone got mad in La Cota at one time or another over stupider things than a bad joke.

In the middle of our castellano lesson, Banban showed up late, as usual, with a strange grin on his face like he could somehow see what was underneath señorita Flores' clothes or something.

Perdón, perdón, he said, and joined his hands together and bowed his head at her, as if begging for forgiveness. We all laughed, but I knew something was up because Banban never apologized for anything.

He sat in the back and kept to himself, paying even less attention to the chalk board than the rest of us. I thought he was probably high again. Banban was always off somewhere else, his mind busy in its own little world. It was one of the reasons people underestimated him. That and the fact that he was the shortest one of all of us. But Banban could beat the shit out of anyone. He knew exactly where to hit where it would hurt the most and didn't hesitate to shatter a bottle of Pepsi in the middle of a brawl and use it to his advantage. I was terrified of him even though he was my best friend.

Once class was over, my stomach rumbled and I walked towards the cantina to buy an empanada. I didn't have any money, but I could always convince this girl Meri to buy me one by telling her she was the most beautiful girl in the liceo. Girls were easy like that. Back then, they still believed the words we said to them. Their hearts were still fresh and pink and hopeful. On the way, Banban pulled me by my arm and took me to a corner behind the water fountain, where all the others were already huddled around waiting for him.

"Todos callados," he said as he unzipped his stained backpack. In that moment, everyone listened.

He reached inside and pulled out a small black revolver that fit neatly into the palm of his hand. It looked tiny. Not like the ones we were used to seeing pulled out in the street, right before we all ran back into our homes and hid under the windows. This gun didn't look like it could hurt anyone, much less put a bullet through someone's body.

"That thing's a toy," said Cucho, vocalizing my own thoughts, even though I knew better than to say them out loud.

"Ah si, you think it's fake?" Banban said, lifting his chin like he usually did when he was fishing for a fight. "Maybe I shoot you in the foot and then you can tell me if you still think it's a toy?"

"Epa, epa," Tairón cut in, the biggest and oldest one of us, our de facto leader. "Banban calmate, just show us the gun."

Banban turned the weapon around. I noticed a small eagle stamped on its face, scratches all over its side. He clicked on something that opened it up. Inside, there were three shiny bullets and three empty holes.

"Where'd you find it?" Jesús asked and his mouth hung open.

"Mi hermano," Banban said, and he started playing with the cylinder, flicking it maniacally with his index finger, making it spin faster and faster, while we all stared at the golden swirl of the bullets going round and round and round.

"Who wants to hold it first?" he asked, and everyone said, "Yo!"

We took turns passing it around, the heavy weight of the gun surprising once it reached our small hands.

"Everyone can hold it except Cucho," Banban declared, and nobody questioned his rule. Cucho sat crossed-legged and watched as Tairón opened it up and took out one of the bullets, rolling it between his index and thumb. During his turn, Jesús grabbed the barrel with the tips of his fingers. Then, he slid his index into the trigger spot and neared it to his face. He squinted one eye as if he were trying to find a target.

I didn't particularly want to touch it, but I knew I had to. If not, they would smell fear on me, and in La Cota, even a whiff of it was dangerous. We'd seen what happened to scared little mariquitos before, they were the ones who got their shoes stolen after school, the ones walking around with no crew. If I didn't grab the gun, I could lose my spot in the circle, and then other kids from other barrios would know I had no one to protect me, and then they'd come after me too.

I held it for a minute and pressed the same button I'd seen Banban hit to open its chamber. I made sure to point the barrel at the floor.

"Why only three bullets?" I asked, and Banban yanked it out of my hand and closed it back up.

"I don't know, Pito," Banban said and threw the gun into his backpack with little care. "You wanna ask my brother what he did with the other ones?"

"Imagine!" Tairón laughed. "He'd probably stick a bullet up Pito's ass," he said, and all the others joined him and started laughing at me, too.

"How long do you have it?" I asked Banban, trying to pretend that I wanted to play around with it a bit longer.

"So many questions," Banban spat at me. "I have it for as long as I want. It's mine now. My brother doesn't need it anymore."

"Let's shoot something," Jesús said, and all of us nodded our heads, even the ones like me who didn't want to. I wanted to go back to class and learn more about tildes and periods and commas and minus and plus signs. I wanted to listen to our teachers sit us down and tell us everything was possible if we just paid attention, how we could make something out of ourselves if we didn't behave like our older brothers, how we could instead be like those people who wore suits on the street and walked into shiny glass buildings in the center of Caracas, buildings we only ever saw from a distance.

Tairón suggested we go to a park far away from La Cota. It was still morning, the sunlight still burning, every inch of our barrio illuminated. We'd be asking for trouble if gun shots started going off around us. We still weren't ready for consequences. No one had pulled a trigger yet. But that was all about to change.

"Vamos," Banban said, and we all stood up and slipped out from the school's front gate easily because no one was ever there to stop us.

The doorbell rang and recess was over. Through the window, I saw señorita Flores writing words on the board and spew chalk dust into the classroom. A ray of light caught the small particles dancing in the air. All five of our desks waited for us, empty.

PATRICIA GARCÍA LUJÁN is a Venezuelan writer based in Miami. Her stories have been published in Blackbird, The Rumpus, Atticus Review, *and* Coolest American Stories 2023. *She's currently at work on a short story collection.*

Hammock

Ikechukwu Roy Udeh-Ubaka

We knew, even before it became news, that the affairs of the occupants of Flat 7B were not straight. Even before Reverend Paul of the Christ Ascension Church stood at the pulpit in his white and green vestments, preaching about the wickedness of men at the hands of one another, his voice booming from the speakers as though he had inanimately stood there and watched it all happen.

We knew.

But before we knew, we watched:

Chinwe in Flat 7A claimed she had first seen the boy arrive with his bag sometime in March.

He always carries a small duffel bag, she said.

Beatrice at 3B said she saw them, Charles and the boy, at the supermarket down the road, carrying a basket full of spaghetti and curries and chicken breasts.

Charles talk say na him brother pikin, she said.

James at 5B ran into them in the yard one early morning, standing beside Charles's car, slightly bent into each other.

They bin dey touch, he said.

Everyone knew a thing or two about the boy's appearance in Hammock, everyone knew a thing or two about everything, but these were the facts: The boy moved in at 11am on Mondays and out at 2pm on Fridays. All before Charles's wife, Amaka, returned on the weekends from her work out of town.

Something else everyone knew: Amaka was the breadwinner, a head nurse at the teaching hospital in Anambra, and Charles was a salesperson with a small company that we all knew yielded him little.

Well, for months and months, the boy came and went.

*   *   *

For context, the boy had a name: Gumption. We never could quite place it right. Who named a child Gumption? Certainly a mother who despised her son. Knew what he would grow into right before she pushed him out of her body and held him against her breasts, or perhaps from when he still occupied her womb. She must have felt a surge rising within her, a sensation that brittled her bones and toppled her across the kitchen table, held her pinned to the wood, her fingers gripping the sides. Preparing her for his arrival.

But Gumption was handsome, the sort that made you squint. From experience, we could all tell that this sort of beauty did not exist without chaos. Chima, the vulcanizer's son had had that sort of beauty, and where was he now? Somewhere off the rails, spending his looks on whoever cared to drop a kobo into his dinner plate. All the Aduke daughters are pregnant or have been married off to men that got them pregnant before they walked down the aisle. And even the new children born with such beauty are taught to hide it, to suppress it, pin it against a stool, and bury their heads in books.

But Gumption was handsome, the sort that made you squint. And we liked this about him. Sometimes, when the power was out, when we gathered in the open balcony on the third floor overlooking the yard, he sat with us, picking chaff out of a tray of beans or riffing through whatever gossip was being marinated that evening while watching the kids play football in the yard. He enjoyed these occasional luxuries, we could tell. It was in the tenderness with which he spoke to Chinwe's daughter; in the way he helped the Adukes in 6B carry up their foodstuffs from the car, running the thin stairs up and down with that boyish flightiness we all recognized and felt, like a person who knew when and how to escape himself.

He was a boy; there was never really a doubt about this. From his choppy frame, newly stubbled cheeks, and that perpetually amused look on his face, we placed him around twenty-three. He seemed a little unformed, out of place.

We also knew Gumption had questions. Every now and again, in the hallway or through the narrow walls of Hammock, we overheard one or two of these questions, and we intently, but seemingly absentmindedly, collected information. He wanted to know why Charles had moved back from America to live here, what the rain in America felt like on his skin. Whether he missed the feeling of inhaling clean air. He wanted to know what the sun felt like on summer mornings. Whether the snow indeed melts in your palm. He wanted to know about Charles's father, his mother, siblings. He wanted to know for how long he had loved men, and for how long he had loved women, and for how long he had been uncertain about his life. He wanted to know why he married his wife.

Charles had met Amaka after he returned to Nigeria, after his visa expired and his application for a permanent residency was denied. They had met at a party at one of his friend's, the way everyone meets anyone anywhere. Amongst a small gathering of friends, Amaka stood by the exit to the balcony, sipping from a glass of wine, her head thrown back in a throaty laugh, her eyes squinting with tears.

His first thought of her wasn't, *This is the woman I will marry.*
It wasn't, *Wow, this is my redemption.*
It simply was: *She has an exciting laugh.*

And coming from a person that hadn't had any proper laughs in a long time, he assumed that something about laughing with her, at her, amongst them, would bring back the laughter that he seemed to have lost in the months since he'd been back.

When he finally spoke to her, it was hours after he had first heard her laugh. He walked up to her where she was standing alone by the bookshelf, her back to him, her gaze on the strings of Soyinka. He imagined her smiling into the titles—recollecting a memory perhaps—but deep down, he hoped she wasn't. Hoped he would be faced with a chance to test his prowess at making her smile.

She was smiling.

Hi, he said, a little too loudly, just as the music was slowing its rhythm.

Hey. She turned to face him, her lips still slashed in a smile. He wanted to ask what made her smile, to share in this amusement that he desperately wanted to get swaddled in.

The party swayed, and so did their conversations. Charles was surprised to find that Amaka too had studied in Philadelphia, and had lived only a few blocks from where he had shared an apartment with some friends. She expressed her surprise that he preferred coffee to tea, called him an Americanah, and jabbed a finger in his chest.

Of course, we had come upon this after the fact. Gumption had told Ahmed in 4A, who had been sort of fucking Luke, who whispered it to Kachi, who had heard it from Ginika. Slowly, the story gathered seasoning; the details were tricky, the certainties muddled, but there was enough to recreate the history of nearly half a decade ago.

When we imagine the rest of that party, they are laughing, breathing into each other's hair, moving their bodies to the rhythm of the night, pressing their lips together, in those liminal spaces between strangers and lovers. But this is mostly speculation, and we do not like to lie.

*　*　*

Think what you must of the occupants of Hammock, but all we ask is that you do not judge us too quickly. We are upstanding people; we can tell you that much for free. We are not like everyone else you've met out there, and this is gospel truth. Yes, we peddle petty gossip about one another, perhaps even lie once or twice to get by. But outwardly, we are smiling, friendly neighbors. We look out for each other beyond the yard, maybe fight once or twice when the situation arises. But we care, and isn't that the most important thing? Like when Chinwe's daughter, Chioma, was slammed against the hard concrete floor and a baby was knocked into her, we all played our parts in rearranging the narrative. Quickly, we came together and found a husband for her, an elderly man who had proved no apparent worry, someone she could sleep with immediately and pin the child on. The Aduke daughters were openly philandering; there was nothing we could do to protect them like we did Chioma. They, too, had had ways to sort themselves out. We had also done the same for Beatrice at 3B, when her husband was caught groping a young girl at the club, bending her over on the dance floor in a manner no respectable married man in his fifties and with a daughter old enough to be the girl's age should. We had helped her move his bags to the storage room one night and helped him put them in a van the next day. Chima, the vulcanizer's son, was a different ballgame. He took to the streets, spreading his mouth as much as he did his legs.

Well, we suppose what we are trying to say is that the affairs of the occupants of Flat 7B weren't exactly a secret at all. They weren't even that discrete. They lingered a little too long by the door of Charles's car and leaned into each other any chance they got. In Hammock, rumors glided through the flats like vines. They crept and stayed on things, waiting for whomever considered them news. But the one person who should have known about Charles and the weekday boy, the one their affair should have mattered the most to, didn't.

Amaka was practically a stranger to us, and this is not to say that we had never spoken to her. She knew us all by name, but you'd be stretching the truth to have called us friends. She smiled cordially when approached in public and returned a greeting whenever she received one, yet carried herself as though it would be a grievance to sit at the corner of the balcony and share a healthy conversation about, perhaps, one of the Aduke daughters.

We did not like her very much.

We tried. We really did. She seemed sweet, leaving every Monday morning and returning every Friday evening in her pristine white garb and those ridiculous nurse hats she pinned to her hair, but if we are being honest, there was some pleasure in bringing her down to one of us, making her aware of the single rupture that could topple her marriage.

So we told her. We were the ones who told her.

All of us. But not all at once. We are better than that.

First, we dropped hints. Ginika whispered it to Chika at the store by the front yard, the whispering just loud enough to be heard if one took the time to listen. Ahmed, who had been sort of fucking Luke told her—giggling, a hand around Luke's shoulder—that Charles was a little like them; family was the word he used. Beatrice said Amaka had not conceived yet because her husband was wasting his semen in the wrong places. *You should come back and keep your marriage. Leave that your work; it will not hold your hands when you're old.*

Each night we dropped a hint, we gathered at the door and listened, our ears pressed to the door. To hear if she would slam the bedroom door, smack Charles across the face, call him a fag. Or maybe she would turn her rage inwards, slam herself against a wall, jump off the balcony, shave off her very own hair. But each night, we returned to our flats one after the other, peddling with us just another relaxed conversation over dinner.

So we decided it was time to be direct, you know, in case she wasn't getting the hints.

Your husband moves a boy into your house while you're at work in Anambra, we said.

They do it in your room, we said.

Right on your matrimonial bed, we said.

We said it again, pointing at their bedroom window.

Her brows came together in a tiny ridge. She looked like we had hoped, ruffled. But then, her brows unfurled, her demeanor straightened, her face unbothered as though we had only spoken of the despicable hike in the price of Garri in the market today. There was, though, on her face, a tiny frown, easy to miss. Later, when Chinwe mentioned it, we all remembered it, took small pleasure in it. The frown, however, seemed from perplexity but not annoyance. Her compressed lips grew firm and obdurate. She thanked us for telling her and went up to her flat. Locked the door and hummed as she set a table for two with Charles.

It was not that we didn't care for Charles. We did. He was a decent guy, one of those people you saw on a regular. You know the kind. The kind with whom you cracked a few jokes, shook hands, but never really thought about. In the two years since they moved into Hammock, Charles barely featured in our conversations, except in reference to Amaka. Of course, until Gumption. He always wore brown corduroy pants and was at the cusp of a bald patch. He was a little thickset, not fat, just what's being called chubby these days, and had a slight stutter that appeared when he seemed wrapped in any crucial emotion. But mostly, he seemed aloof, removed somewhat, like a person quietly mourning.

Listen, what we are trying to say is that we didn't consider Charles at the time. Okay, maybe a little, but poking Amaka was the goal, and we couldn't allow such things interfere with that.

*   *   *

It's hard to say exactly what happened, but this was what we remembered: It was a particularly hot August day. The brilliant sun pouring down its rays on the earth like molten rain. A day on which the very outlines of Hammock shuddered as if in protest at the heat. Heat radiating from the banisters on balconies, and the glass from the windows throwing out a blinding radiance. Whatever small breeze there was seemed like the breath of a flame fanned by slow bellows.

So, you're the boy fucking my husband, was all she said when she walked into the flat.

It was a Thursday, this we can say for sure because it was the day the power supply management came to disconnect the light, and the unfortunate man who climbed the pole left with a trail of blood blinding his eyes from an unseen slingshot. It was a Thursday because it was the day Zara in 2B had her increasingly frustrating piano lessons. It was a Thursday because it wasn't the day Amaka should have been back.

There must have been shock on his face. Oh, poor Gumption. He must have stood still, his feet sinking into the grey carpets, praying for a hole to bore beneath him and swallow him. He must have peed a little in his trousers; in our imagination he did. We would've.

From the door, we'd listened to Gumption attempt to speak, explain himself, but nothing came. Amaka sat herself down by the dining table, watching. She must have sized him up, imagining what it was he could give her husband that she couldn't.

James, peeping from the keyhole said the boy pulled up a chair and sat facing her, and it was clear there wasn't anything either of them could say to remedy the moment.

Soon, we returned to our flats, to the balcony picking weevils out of a tray of beans, to the children playing football in the yard downstairs, to the noise of Zara's increasingly frustrating piano lesson.

About half an hour later, we all watched him leave, his duffel bag hanging from his arm, his face weary and tired, and something else. He left without looking back, and we already missed him a little.

That night, Amaka made love to Charles in a manner we believe she had never before. She moaned, loudly, pressed her fingers deep into his back, flipped over, let him take her from behind. We like to believe this was her way of keeping her marriage, as Chinwe had once advised. Of course, we hadn't known any of this, it was simply what Chinwe reported back to us.

*   *   *

By and by the weeks went. August gave way to September with its hectic rush of rowdiness and crowded streets, and children returning to school. Rain vanished and the sun took hold of the sky, its irksomeness blinding and inexplicably disturbing. And all along, Hammock bristled with tattle. Chima, the vulcanizer's son, had once again brought shame upon us. He was found in a dark alley fumbling the penis of one of those useless street urchins he was sure to be found around and was beaten and paraded around the street, and finally abandoned by the exit gate. The youngest Aduke daughter had mirrored her sisters' footsteps and became pregnant and another wedding was looming. James had lost his job at the whole food factory because he was caught lifting too much of the leftovers, and a young, attractive couple had moved into 2B, all rosey and bubbly.

So, you see, we became occupied with other things. Important things were happening in Hammock, and news was only news for so long, so we moved on. The affairs of 7B gave way for more immediate gist, and even when Gumption returned, we didn't think too much of it. He sat amongst us, and we filled him in on the happenings in the month since he had been away.

His routine remained the same: moved in Monday morning and out Friday afternoon. Gumption, it appeared, still retained the ability to secure the things he wanted even in the face of opposition, and in utter disregard for the convenience and desire of others. About him, there was some quality, hard and persistent, with the strength and endurance of rock, that it seemed could not be beaten down or ignored. Yet, on closer observation, when he sat around with us on the balcony, we could sense a slight shift in his demeanor, something we all recognized as caution.

We wondered for how long this would go on without Amaka's awareness, if we should tell her again. Considered it for a day, maybe more, discussed it amongst ourselves, but the satisfaction we had previously hoped for hadn't been met, and as we said, we are upstanding people. We liked Gumption, at least he was one of us.

So we didn't tell her.

For weeks and weeks, he came and went.

*   *   *

It rained on the Wednesday Amaka returned, generous slashes soaking the earth, carrying with it the late November breeze. As she climbed the stairs to her flat, Amaka's ivory face was what it always was, beautiful and caressing. Or maybe today a little masked. Unrevealing. Unaltered and undisturbed by any emotions within or without. A small crowd gathered along the stairwell as she ascended the stairs to the top of the building where her flat was. We had always sensed that there was an amazing soft malice about her, hidden well away until provoked, like a person capable of biting, and very effectively too. We had never seen her react with any visceral emotion—she always had a plain smile on her face, never laughing too hard or frowning too sternly—but if history was any indication, we knew that a person who never wore their emotions outwardly was capable of much more destruction.

We waited till she was inside her flat to gather by her door. There was no sound. Not a single word was heard. There was the occasional click of her box-heeled shoes against the tiled floors, and then something that sounded like the shattering of glass in a sink.

From the keyhole, we took turns watching Gumption gather his things. Amaka sat on the sofa and said nothing. Within the hour, he was gone, and there was a finality to this departure we knew was definite. He turned and waved at us. He stared up at the browning walls of Hammock, up at the window of Flat 7B, shook his head and left.

The weekend went by with them laughing in the hallway. There, walking the hallway, were our favorite couple, Amaka whispering into Charles's ear, nibbling his neck. His hand over her shoulders. There was something in their stride that made us smile, curious, and just a little jealous. They had worked on things without involving others, without creating a scene. She seemed determined to keep him. Her freshly glossed lips lifted at the corners to form a smile. Truly, she was above us all. It surprised us how intent she was on holding fast the outer shell of her marriage, on keeping her life fixed, certain. Brought to the edge of this distasteful reality, her fastidious nature did not recoil. It was as though she needed us to see that she—they—were trudging forward, regardless.

So it did not surprise us at all on Monday morning when we saw her put her usual bag into her trunk, her hair wrapped in a neat bun under her hat and clutching her tote. She stood by the car, looked up at her bedroom window, waved, started the car and drove away.

*   *   *

There had been no need to involve the police, no reason for us to cause that sort of scene in Hammock. Monday went and Tuesday followed, and the door to Flat 7B remained shut. On Thursday, Chinwe found the body. The smell had reached through the walls, wrapped itself around her living room, and seeped into sheets. James from 5B broke down the door. The house smelled of death. The medics came and flipped the body on a gurney. We stood by the entrance to the flat, snapping our fingers, damning it all.

The following day, Amaka returned. We had aired out the apartment, emptied spray cans of air fresheners and Dettol. We left the windows open and wrapped a piece of cloth around the handle of the door to hold it shut. Chinwe kept watch through the day because we know how these children like to steal.

Amaka sat on the sofa and remained quiet, staring ahead at the hideous Yoruba print on the wall across the room.

We came in singly, Chinwe from 7A, then Uju from 4B, then James from 5B. Soon, we filled up the living room, sitting on the sofa beside her, on the side stools, on the floor.

Amaka—soft faced, dark hair, pinched lips, forlorn eyes—seemed too tired, too shocked, utterly weary, and violently removed.

The room was quiet, except for the occasional sorrys and take hearts and this too shall pass.

Someone said that the doctor had ruled it a heart attack. Someone else said that he had been dressed like he was going to work.

And then she began to cry rackingly, her entire body heaving with convulsive sobs. She tried to speak but choked, her voice turning into a whimper like a hurt child's. Chinwe laid a hand on her shoulder in a soothing gesture. In those few seconds, Amaka seemed to age.

She moaned and sank down on the sofa. Moaned again and shut her eyes like she had gone to sleep.

In the same manner we came, we left, returned to our daily routines, gathering at the balcony on the third floor to talk and watch the children play football. And yet we knew, we were certain of it: she had done it. There was no use debating it; we knew.

You remember she's a nurse, one of us said.

Even dressed him like he was going to work, another said.

She did it, we all agreed.

We knew, and yet knew that nothing would come from our knowing. It was not a secret, but it was not information that could result in anything either. The day went by, the sun oranged and receded behind the clouds. Once or twice, one of us remembered Charles or Amaka or Gumption, and we shook our heads and sucked our teeth, and then the moment passed and life continued.

The next day, Amaka dumped two boxes and a duffel bag in the backseat of her car and drove off before the sun rose.

A month later, we gathered money together and held a wake for Charles. The wake was simple, the dancers danced, the drummers drummed, the caterers catered, but none of us cried. As sad as it was, none of us qualified to cry, to grieve this loss. Charles was not ours to mourn, and the only person who could have mourned him was not there.

ROY is a fiction MFA student at the University of Florida, and a 2018 alumnus of the Purple Hibiscus Creative Writers Workshop taught by Chimamanda Ngozi Adichie. He is also the 2022 winner for the Gerald Kraak Award. His works and interviews have appeared in McSweeney's Quarterly, Wasafiri, Bakwa Magazine, Lolwe, *and The Gerald Kraak Anthology. In 2019, he was named by Electric Literature as "One of the Most Promising New Voices of Nigerian Fiction."*

Sanctuary

Tim Griffith

I

Duncan paused a moment in his posthole digging and wiped his brow. Before him the pastures rolled gently down—dry stone walls separating each off from the next—then came the bay in a half mile or so, then the sands of the islands, shimmering like gold. A few yards behind, Mark sat on the truck and hummed as he fiddled around with a coil of copper wiring.

With the hole deep and wide enough, Duncan picked a cedar post off the ground and dropped it in, jiggled it around and got it level before backfilling the dirt. He took the drill and drove two ceramic insulators into the wood, one at chest height and the other at waist height, then tested the post's strength before moving on.

More than five miles remained but the sun was already low and the clouds were gathering. Just as he began at the earth to start on the next hole, a curtain of rain touched down on the beach and began up through the pastures. He turned to look at Mark, who had hopped off the tailgate and was staring at the coming rain. The old man couldn't see well enough to read the newspaper or legally drive a vehicle, but it had taken Duncan a week and a half to notice—he was that good at concealing his burden, that determined to carry on.

"We're about to be soaked," Mark said.

"It's already raining by the shore."

"We'll beat it home, save this for later."

Duncan was grateful to Mark and his wife Addy for offering him the job, and he was feeling stronger, his mind beginning to sharpen too—he'd be a normal person again before too long, plain and boring as anyone else. They provided him a bed in the attic and three meals a day. He loved it out here in the country, so far removed from his troubles.

It was a rescue, really, not a farm as they'd told him: two dozen horses and a donkey lived here, roaming and grazing without obligation or fear. Mark's life was focused entirely on his animals now—making sure they had enough feed and pasture to go about their business as comfortably as possible—but as a younger man, before an acute case of glaucoma stole the better part of his sight, he'd been an architect at a Boston firm. It must have been dreadful, the early days before he truly came to terms with his new reality.

Duncan set the tools in the truck bed, placed a hand on Mark's shoulder and said, "Let me drive for a change."

"That clutch is hard to get the hang of."

"I'll just grind the gears then," Duncan said. "Someday a horse is going to trot out in front of you, ruin your whole week."

"I see their shapes well enough," Mark said. "But fine."

He climbed into the driver's seat beside Mark, started the engine and drove up toward the farmhouse. Soon the pastures were behind them and they entered a hardwood forest, stunted by sea spray, where the road was rutted deeply, muddy with snowmelt. Duncan tried to turn out from the ruts to approach the barn but the tires caught in the grooves and the truck moved forward at a sideways slide for a moment; then the treads found something to grip and the vehicle lurched free of the ruts onto higher ground, and Duncan drove through a field toward the main gravel drive.

"We'll park it in the barn tonight," Mark said as they approached. "Won't even put the tools away." He got out and slid open the corrugated metal doors.

Duncan drove in as two chickens jumped down from the hayloft, startled by the sputtering old engine, and scrambled to a horse stall near the back. He parked toward the middle and set the brake, put the truck into gear to be sure it wouldn't roll if a horse were to use it as an itching post. When he got out Mark was already peeling strips of hay off a bale and pitchforking them to a hay crib. Duncan took another fork from the wall and began to help, and within ten minutes they had filled all the cribs in the barn.

The two men closed up the barn for the night, leaving the back entrance open for the horses as usual. The incoming clouds were a dark, ominous blue, but the sun shone beneath them and flooded the new growth on the trees in a strange light. The budding leaves appeared more vibrant than usual, almost neon in hue, as if they themselves were producing the glow, rather than the sun. A thin rain began to fall as they plodded toward the farmhouse but a rainbow wouldn't show. By the time they reached the doorstep the smell of stew was thick in the air—red wine, onions and thyme, the venison a neighbor had brought by that very morning. They were glad to be done for the day.

*   *   *

The nights were hard for Duncan still, now six months clean and sober. He would often lie awake listening to the house groan as the wind pulled at its sides, and to the coyotes who raised their voices in the darkness. Addy's cats seemed to howl whenever a peaceful quiet took hold too, though Duncan knew they were fine, only wanted to be let outside.

One night with a full moon Duncan found himself awake like this. He read a book and rolled around trying to get comfortable but it was of no use; finally, he looked out his window and saw Addy standing in the field with her bow, firing arrows high into a distant grove of trees. At first, he thought he was dreaming, it didn't seem real. She was plucking arrows from a five-gallon bucket set beside her, notching them in the thread and pulling back, smooth and easy. He watched for the time it took her to shoot off a dozen arrows, then pulled on his pants and jacket and headed outside.

It was colder than he'd thought it would be but dry, not the kind of wet cold that had been gnawing at his bones for weeks. He smelled the smoke from the woodstove and saw the wispy string of it cutting at the sky like a scar, and soon came to within earshot of Addy where he called out softly so as not to startle her.

"I saw you practicing," he explained. "I thought a walk might clear my head."

"I must look like a crazy person." She glanced at Duncan briefly and widened her eyes at him before reaching into the bucket for another arrow. The fletching was at her ear in an instant, then she released the arrow and it whooshed off into the night.

"I guess anyone would want to give it a try if they had all this land."

"Be my guest." She offered the bow to him.

"I'm afraid of them, to tell you the truth. It's always seemed like something might go wrong, that the arrow might end up sticking out from my eye."

"Well, that's silly of you." She continued to fire off rounds as she spoke: "Mark used to do this with me when he could see better. He still lets me guide him sometimes, but he wouldn't want to have someone else catch him at it. My father used to do this at night too, you know—it's not like I came up with the idea. Makes you feel like an archer in the Middle Ages, protecting some keep or another. To hell with targets."

"Don't you worry about hitting a horse?"

"They can't get over there," she said, then she pointed to the sky. "See that bright star, the top of that skinny triangle? If I'm perfect, exactly the same each and every time, the arrows will be bunched up together when I collect them. And if I did this long enough, they'd spread out to an arc that matched the path of that star. That's if I had enough arrows—which I don't—and if there weren't all those branches in the way—which there are."

Addy fired another arrow and it curled up toward the star, and though Duncan couldn't hear it crashing through the trees he knew it surely had. He looked up at the stars and got the urge to climb into his car and drive very far away, though he couldn't say where he would want to go. He thought of a few places he'd always wanted to visit and it depressed him even more, imagining himself traveling to them alone.

"You must be going stir-crazy," Addy said. She'd finished off the bucket, and the two of them began to walk toward the farmhouse. "You wouldn't have come out to watch me if you could bear that attic a moment longer."

"I'm not sure why I can't sleep," he said. "I guess I'm used to the cars in town."

"Just you wait till the frogs crawl out from their holes and begin to sing in a few weeks or so. They'll drown out everything else. You'll sleep like a baby boy."

* * *

During the workweek Addy would always prepare a simple breakfast for Mark and Duncan. She'd set toast and butter and jam on the table, brew a pot of coffee, leave the milk and sugar on the counter. She brought in the paper from the top of the driveway too until Duncan caught on and began to head out early to save her the trip. She'd helped guide Mark through life for the past thirty years—since he'd been forced to relinquish his driver's license—and he needed her greatly, despite his resolve.

She did all this while working as a fourth-grade teacher at Westport Elementary, and on weekends she worked more still, now alongside her husband—with the animals in the fields, in the forest bucking firewood, at the agricultural supply store buying feed and new equipage, and so on. It was on just such a morning, a Sunday in the middle of May, when she had her stroke. She'd been moving through life at leisurely pace—not without its trials and heartache, though easily enough all told—but now that would change forever.

"Bruce and Blue snuck onto the beach again," Mark said as he slid on his muck boots. "I heard him braying on the wind through the bathroom window."

"Those two morons," Addy said. "I'll shoo them up to the rest."

Blue was Addy's favorite horse of the whole herd. She stood seventeen hands high and was shiny and black as a judge in gown, and of all the horses they had she was Bruce's only ally and stuck by him with constant devotion. Addy thought it was about the most darling thing in the world, that old draft horse following her little donkey wherever he went and gnashing her teeth if the other horses gave him trouble—they were as good as husband and wife.

Mark and Duncan continued their work trimming the horses' hooves as Addy took the footpath down through the woods to the beach. She carried a single lead and a few carrots, knowing that was all she needed to shepherd the two animals up through the fields to the barn. She whistled as she walked and listened to the birds calling, then heard a sudden thud and watched as two birds fell to the ground right before her. One of them flew off immediately, but the other sat dazed in the fallen leaves that blanketed the trail. It was a grackle, its feathers sparkling with iridescence as they caught the sun just so. Addy knew it would be okay in a short while—the bird hadn't even been knocked out fully and was only a little weak for the time being. She left it where it sat and walked on.

Bruce and Blue were up the beach from where the trail fed into it, small as toys to Addy and out on a rocky point with a group of deer. They seemed to be getting along fine with the wildlife as they licked salt from the rocks and the mounds of seaweed. About five miles out to sea, halfway to Cuttyhunk Island, a scallop trawler chugged slowly by.

As she started up the beach for the point the deer caught her scent on the breeze and darted their eyes, then were off leaping into the forest in no time, their cottony tails snapping about like whips in the thicket. Bruce and Blue smelled her as well, but they began toward her in excitement. Addy and Mark's animals were fond of people in a way that most livestock are not; they had nothing to fear and came when called, and they would just as soon sleep on the living room rug if it were allowed of them.

"Bluebell!" Addy called. "Bruce Caboose!"

They picked up their pace to a cantor, whinnying and hawing, tossing their heads in joy. They came to an abrupt stop right in front of Addy and waited as she pulled the carrot out from her jacket. She felt strangely breathless after calling out to them and a thought, so simple it consisted only of the word carrot, swirled about through her head. She couldn't think of anything else for some reason, but it didn't bother her, not yet. She held the carrot in her hand but it fell to the ground, and Bruce, the shorter and greedier of the two animals, bent down to snatch it. Addy watched Bruce crunch the carrot in his mouth as Blue tried to steal it from him. She remembered the grackle hopping around on the leaves but couldn't say what it was anymore—it was only a curious, nameless thing to her now.

In her mind she watched a volley of tiny arrows pierce the grackle's neck, then she saw the scallop trawler again and her husband was on it, waving to her as he spun the wheel. There was a young man standing beside him, but who was he? And how on earth could they ever know the way? They were gliding smoothly across the water, but soon the boat dipped beneath the waves and out of view, and Addy wanted to weep.

"Help them," she whispered. "Help them."

Then she fell to her knees and set her face in the sand, and all she could think was, *help them*, for an endless stretch of time. It was all that she knew for certain.

*   *   *

At lunchtime Mark and Duncan decided to drive down to the beach to see what was keeping Addy. They had trimmed the hooves of six horses, and an old BLM mare Mark had bought at an auction out West had kicked Duncan in the stomach. Both men were exhausted, covered in straw and manure. Duncan drove the little truck down through the pastures, past the fencing they had erected a month prior and over the ruts still slick from recent rainfall. He parked the truck close to the beach and they got out and walked a short ways, coming to the water on the opposite end of the point from Addy. Neither she nor the animals were visible to them, but they walked to the point to peek around the bend just to be sure.

When they got to the point Duncan could see Addy and the two animals about a hundred yards off. "It looks like they're all lying in the sand together," he said.

"That's not right," Mark muttered.

In an instant they both knew something terrible had happened. Duncan ran ahead of Mark, who stumbled along as fast as he could manage. Bruce stood up from the ground as Duncan came upon them and shook the sand off his sides, but Addy and Blue remained motionless. Duncan bent down to Addy, found her eyes drooped halfway shut with dried blood fanned out from her nose, spreading over her face and neck.

"There's been some kind of accident!" he shouted.

Mark tripped on a rock and fell just a few yards from his wife, then crawled over to her and put his hands gently on her face.

"What's the matter?" he cried. "What's happened?"

"I'm going to get the truck," Duncan told him.

Though there was no way for them to know, the horse had died of a heart attack soon after Addy fell to the sand—a wild, outrageous coincidence, and now it looked as if Addy had been injured by the horse somehow, kicked in the head or thrown off her back. It didn't make sense to the two men who had come upon her like this, but that wasn't something to ponder now—they had to get her to a hospital. Duncan sprinted back to the truck and started it up. He drove onto the beach and raced toward Mark and Addy, pulled beside them. The two men cleared everything out from the bed and lifted Addy up onto it without so much as voicing a single word. She was laid out flat and Mark climbed in with her; he kneeled beside her and tried to hold her head steady once they got going.

They drove up to the farmhouse with the donkey galloping behind them, and then they decided it best to drive right on by, to keep going straight for the small fire station five miles up the road. They pulled up to the giant doors of the station, hopped out and started slamming their palms and fists against them, screaming at the top of their lungs. Out the firemen poured—some wearing shorts or sweatpants, others with only half their uniforms on—

and Duncan sat on a curb as Addy was loaded into the ambulance with Mark right behind her.

II

Awhile before all this, Duncan's mother had died—a slow, torturous battle with breast cancer that eventually proved too much for her—and in the following months he had reconnected with some of his high school buddies, spent the better part of a year using heroin again. He got set on a course that might well have killed him, but his father finally intervened and dragged him off to a fancy addiction recovery center in Vermont. And then this job came up, which he endured at first but became quite invested in after only a few weeks.

Today, as with every day now, he had to drive Mark an hour north to the outskirts of Boston, where Abby was healing at her rehabilitation center. He turned into the facility's driveway and wound up the hill through the grand oaks, elms and horse chestnuts, found a parking spot, then took Addy's box of magazines and books from the trunk and walked with Mark toward the center. In unfamiliar places, Mark carried an old ski pole with him, the leather strap wrapped around his wrist; if a person didn't know any better, they'd think he used it for a walking stick rather than as a tool to help him see the world by.

They entered the old ivy-covered building, and in the halls and common rooms was the usual crowd: a few younger people with traumatic brain injuries in the company of many elderly people who had suffered strokes and other such devastations. They struggled behind walkers and stood upright with the aid of railings and caught their breath on plush leather chairs in between. Mark and Duncan took the elevator up to Addy's floor and found her in her wheelchair, sunlight slanting through the window onto her lap as a nurse braided her hair. The nurse looked fresh out of college—she still had braces even—and she giggled at Addy's jokes and gazed with genuine admiration at her.

"My two boys have come to see me," Addy said. She shook her head and put a hand over her eyes and added, "My God, I sound old."

She had a slight droop to her mouth on the left-hand side but apart from that her face had lifted back to normal. The rest of her, though, that was going to take a lot more work. The doctors told her she would probably walk again one day, though she would need a cane to help her do it. Her left arm had withered considerably, and she'd never get the use of her left leg just right. She would have to swing it by the hip to take each step; even a crack in the sidewalk might trip her up, they said, so she would have to be careful.

The nurse soon left the room. Mark came behind Addy and kissed the back of her head; he released the brakes to her wheelchair and they began out through the doorway. Duncan followed them down the hall and into the elevator, past all the patients on the first floor and out to the warmth of the afternoon.

"It's funny about the girl," Addy said after they'd picked a nice spot in the shade. "She's from Westport originally, would you believe it? I had her as a student about fifteen years ago. She recognized me first, then it all came back."

She slid a folder out from the space beside her in the wheelchair and set it onto her lap. She found the reading notes she'd written up the night before and asked Duncan to take out his copy of *The Odyssey*, which they had begun just a few days earlier. They started right in, discussing Penelope and the throngs of suitors come to Ithaca to wed her. It had been a few weeks since these lessons began, since soon after Addy relearned her speech and it was clear that her recovery was progressing smoothly. Duncan had suggested something like this after she'd explained how deeply she missed her students, and then they'd started a sort of guided reading group together in which Addy led the two men in discussion. It also meant that Duncan would read aloud to Mark for about an hour each night, a ritual that had been awkward in the beginning but now seemed to comfort them both.

They discussed the beginnings of the book for nearly an hour, and once Addy felt they had covered enough ground, she suddenly said, "You must know who I'm going to ask about now...how's the old boy holding up?"

"Still finding his way," Mark said. "Getting on with a few of the mares."

"Well, I miss him."

She was speaking of Bruce, the lone donkey in that herd of powerful horses. She had begun to worry about him almost immediately after she awoke. Before she could even voice a word, Mark had put a pen into her right hand—her good one, though she'd been left-handed before—and she had scrawled out the donkey's name in a wobbly script. When Mark asked her what she wanted to know, she wrote, *He's a widower now, his wife died.*

It soon came out that Addy believed the old horse had saved her life, had offered up a piece of her soul as she lay on the beach in the throes of death that day. *I can feel her galloping through me,* she wrote. *She's a part of me now.* And it was curious to Mark and Duncan later on, because they soon learned that Addy had already lost consciousness when Blue died beside her. She hadn't seen the horse fall, she told them, but somewhere deep within her mind—or perhaps someplace else—she had watched Blue trotting slowly away from her into a strange field, and she had known not to follow.

*   *   *

June was drier than usual that year and July was too, and by August the ponds were nothing but mud puddles. Mark and Duncan went on with everything as well as they could: They began before dawn most days, their headlamps slicing the darkness, shining back to them off the eyes of wildlife—foxes and coyotes, owls and nighthawks—and showing them the way. There was always fencing to mend, hay to cut and bale, brush along the pastures to trim back, and with two new foals Mark wanted to get out to the herd each day to check them over too. By noon, they had usually put in six or seven hours. They would end their day at lunchtime, then drive the hour up to Boston, where Addy would be waiting.

They made their way through the ancient poem as Addy had asked of them, and they discussed it each afternoon with her unless something came up that denied it. In the nights Duncan read to Mark on the back porch, the mosquito zapper buzzing and popping above them, and it always happened that a number of horses would hear their chatter and come up from the fields to investigate. The animals would sit in the fine dirt around the porch and roll around now and then, seeming to Duncan as if they were his children and he was lulling them to sleep with a fairytale. Bruce was always there too. He would sit off to the side, his legs tucked under his body in a way that made it look like he had no legs at all. He often brayed when Duncan and Mark finished their reading for the evening, but after some discussion they resolved never to tell Addy about this—they were sure it would only have upset her.

*   *   *

One morning Duncan woke up and he didn't know where he was. The afternoon sun shone on his face and a bird hopped about nearby, its red cheek feathers and mottled wings making it seem like some errant species from the tropics. It flew off with three quick flaps followed by a long glide, its call high and piercing in the distance.

His throat was on fire. He threw up on a patch of dry moss, then recalled bits of the evening. He'd started thinking about his mother and had bought a pint of whiskey at the liquor store, drank the whole thing driving the backroads in a hateful mood and passed out a few hundred yards into the woods in a place he didn't even recognize. He was lucky he hadn't crashed his car and gotten arrested, lucky too that he hadn't gone to New Bedford to buy a bag of dope—at least he had that to be grateful for.

Mark must have waited for him all morning. The old man could make do on the farm, but the drive up to see Addy was impossible on his own. Duncan stood up and brushed the dirt from his back. He tried to get his bearings—he could hear the ocean in one direction, a woman singing in the other. He walked toward the woman's voice and soon came to the edge of a yard, where he found a summer cottage with a roof of weathered shingles surrounded by vegetable beds bursting with tomato plants, melons, and sweet peas. The gray hair of an old woman's head was visible above the wooden blinds of an outdoor shower; she was singing beautifully, completely unabashed and free. He finally came to a drive and walked away from her lovely voice, feeling slightly better about things, the possibilities of life.

When he arrived at the farm Mark was sitting on the porch steps eating a ham sandwich and drinking a beer. "He's alive," Mark said with a chuckle, then wiped his mouth clean with a bandanna. "I've decided you're allotted one missed day without notice per season."

"I slept in the woods last night," Duncan said. "Right in the dirt beneath a tree."

Mark convinced Duncan to eat a little something so he ate a pickle and drank a glass of milk. Then they left for the rehabilitation center, though they would arrive later than usual. Duncan told Mark about his night as he drove, the old man listening thoughtfully. Mark had never asked much about Duncan's past before, and Duncan had never asked much about his either. But Duncan went through everything now—how he hadn't spent enough time with his mother toward the end because he couldn't bear to see her, how he'd then dealt with his guilt by dulling his senses, the only way he knew how. They were halfway to Boston when he finally quieted down. Mark didn't speak for a long time afterward.

Finally, the old man said, "I used to design houses when I was younger—summerhouses for Wall Street men on the Cape and Islands mostly."

"I knew you were an architect," Duncan said. "You told me that once."

"Well, I was pretty damn good at it, one of the best around, and then when I couldn't see anymore I almost wanted to put an end to things. I stopped seeing my friends and it got to be that I would break down crying whenever Addy left my side. I couldn't figure out what to do with myself. It was awful, those first few years.

"We moved into an apartment right off Harvard Square, thinking I could learn my way around and get where I needed to go without any trouble. I figured out the neighborhood alright, but I was just wandering about. I took piano lessons, somehow thought I might turn into Ray Charles if I concentrated every bit of my mind on it." He laughed quietly and added, "It doesn't work that way, unfortunately...I could hardly play a nursery rhyme."

Duncan looked at Mark and wasn't sure what he was getting at, what sort of lesson this was supposed to be. He knew that losing the better part of his sight so suddenly must have been a true nightmare, but the old man seemed so capable now. He rarely considered how difficult that journey might have been.

"So now you have horses," Duncan offered after a while, and Mark glanced over at him, his eyes a marbled blue. He had a look on his face that seemed to say, *You've got me. You've uncovered the secret.*

"So now I have horses," he repeated.

III

Addy was coming home in October, but only for an afternoon since she still couldn't be away from care for very long. She was excited to see the animals, to see how the place had changed since she'd been away. It was five full months out and she had made much progress. She was beginning to go stir-crazy at the center, where friends had come and gone and new ones had joined the ranks and begun their recoveries too.

"I'm trying to decide what I'll do," she said a few weeks before her homecoming. "I might want to go down to the beach where it happened—confront it head on—or maybe I'll just sit with the cats all afternoon. That would do me good."

"I'm not sure how we'd get you down to the beach," Mark said.

"That's right, that's right," she laughed. "I forget why I'm here sometimes."

"Well, we've built a nice ramp for you that goes straight up to the living room," Duncan told her. "You won't have any trouble with it."

"A wheelchair ramp?" She sighed at that. "You're too good to me."

They'd built it the day before, and it would do for a single visit though they weren't too happy with the final product. They had pulled dozens of spare planks from the barn, separated those that were unbowed from the rest and cut them to equal lengths. Perhaps it should have been a joyful task, a sign of better days to come, but it was grim work for them both.

Duncan picked out the five planks that looked best and laid them flat on the driveway, bridged them together using two-by-fours as crossbeams. Once that was completed, they carried the ramp over to the front steps and propped it in place so the end was flush with the doorjamb. They then spent the better part of an hour fitting brick and cinderblock underneath for support. Mark paused as they made the final adjustments. He rubbed his index finger with his thumb, held it up close to his eye.

"It's a telephone pole," Duncan said after taking a look. "A whole tree."

He went inside and came back out with a pair of tweezers. Mark held his hand out and Duncan took hold of it. The splinter was buried deep and required some digging to remove, but Mark stayed absolutely still, taking in the day around him. Finally, the splinter slid free and it was long and gnarled in the prongs.

"My God," Mark said as he wove his fingers over his eyes. "How will she ever get into the bathroom? That somehow slipped my mind."

"It won't be so hard," Duncan said. "We can figure that out later."

"It's not just that. She won't be able to do a thing. She can't live here anymore, that's for certain. We'll have to move to assisted living, so long to everything we've built together."

"How can you say that?" Duncan asked. "You aren't thinking straight."

Mark turned from Duncan and walked up the ramp, checking its stability with light bounces on the balls off his feet. When he entered the house, he clicked on the radio and a game show was playing, witty comedians and academics joking about the provenance of odd words, politics and pop culture, all at once it seemed.

Duncan wanted to rush inside and shake some sense into the old man but he couldn't blame him for losing faith. Instead, he walked up the driveway and looked out over a field that had yet to be cut for the second time that year. The horses were fenced off from the field, but out in the middle of it, Bruce was moving slowly—he'd snuck under the lines as he often did. He walked through the waist-high alfalfa like a seal basking in the surface waters with only his head and back visible, the shoots of green and purple rolling around him in the breeze like seaweed as he happily mowed them down. It made Duncan smile in spite of things, to see the donkey being bad, out feasting on the coming winter's silage.

*   *   *

A few days later Duncan sat in the grass beside Bruce, scratching the donkey's enormous ears. Mark had decided they could take the day off and was lying on the couch in the living room, listening to the news. Duncan had tried to sleep in but could hardly stay under the covers much past dawn. He remembered the night he saw Addy shooting arrows into the trees and hoped her left arm would heal up strong so she could do it again someday.

Those same woods stretched out before him. It was odd that he'd never spent any time in them—he'd been to almost every corner of the farm by then. All he had to do was walk the breadth of the pasture and he'd be in them, the fall leaves crunching underfoot. He got up and started across the field. Bruce stood up and followed behind him, and they walked in close file together, the frost wetting both Duncan's shoes and Bruce's hooves alike so they each kicked off tiny beads of dew with each stride.

They came to the woods, where it was dark and peaceful. Duncan decided he'd retrieve an arrow or two—she couldn't possibly have found them all over the years—and only an instant passed before he saw one slanted into the soil. He pulled it out and examined its rusted shaft and tattered fletching, then he saw another a few steps from the first, stuck a half foot into a rotten log. This is it, he thought, this is where she bunched up the arrows one night, then forgot to collect them. But he saw another a bit farther and more still, and soon he took in the whole forest anew and saw that they were everywhere, hundreds, or perhaps even thousands of them. They were spread about evenly, every couple of feet or so.

He stood there, shocked and saddened, trying to figure out what this could mean. He thought of Mark and how everything had changed for Addy when he lost his sight. She'd lived in a city her whole adult life up till that point, and maybe she'd never wanted this farming life in the first place. He thought of her guiding Mark as he shot the arrows, assuring him she'd fetch them in the morning when she knew full well she'd never get around to it.

Everyone has a place like this, he thought, and most of us can hardly make it through the day without going there at least once. He decided he wouldn't ask her about the arrows when she came back...she could keep it, this secret grove where she sent her sorrow.

*   *   *

The day finally came for Addy to return home for the afternoon. Mark had called friends and family members from as far away as New Hampshire and Maine to come celebrate this milestone with her. They would have a clambake as they used to do when they were younger. Duncan and Mark borrowed a van from a neighbor that could accommodate Addy and her wheelchair. They drove up to the rehabilitation center and found her sitting just outside the entrance, bundled up in winter clothes though it was quite warm for that time of year. Beside her, an elderly man was hunched over his walker as he smoked a cigarette. He smiled at Mark and Duncan, telling them to bring her back in one piece because they were actually somewhat fond of the old girl around here.

"I couldn't sleep a wink last night," she said as they pushed her to the van. "I was afraid I'd wake up and it wouldn't be true. I'd be just coming back around from my long sleep, and I'd have to do all that hard work a second time over."

They helped her into the front seat of the van so she wouldn't get carsick. Even that small movement was something of a trial, but they got her in and made it to the highway, were cruising the back roads in just over an hour.

"It's actually a bit upsetting to see this town again," Addy said suddenly.

"You've been gone a long time," Duncan reminded her.

They passed the old general store and the spillway that everyone called Coca-Cola Falls due to its brown, tannin-rich waters. Lines of stone walls arced over hayfields on either side of the road. They were almost home, just a few minutes more. Addy fidgeted around in her seat and seemed to grow more and more flustered as they neared. The dead leaves trembled like withered fingers on the trees. They passed a farmer sitting on the bucket seat of his tractor, a baler pulled along behind him through the fields, pushing out hay and cutting it into blocks again and again. There a horse rolled in the dust, there a neighbor out for her morning stroll smiled and waved, gave a thumbs up at the sight of Addy in the passenger seat.

"This isn't right," she said. "It all seems changed around, everything's on the wrong side of the road for me." She began to cry softly into her forearm.

"Nothing's different," Mark said. "It's another season, that's all."

They made it to the intersection of their long, dead-end road, where Addy told Duncan to turn left as if he didn't know the way. "It's like I've been gone for half my life," she said. "The whole town is new. I feel it's been torn down and built again, but all of it flawed and warped and misshapen somehow. I doubt the horses will even recognize me."

"You'll just need some time to get used to it again," Mark said.

Now she was weeping in great, heaving sobs. They pulled into the top of the driveway and Mark got out of the van to retrieve the newspaper. He got back in, put his hands on Addy's shoulders and whispered something into her ear. She laughed, a desperate chuckle, then said she was a queen returning home, though—not a king.

The driveway was long before them and wended through the trees like the meandering wake of a motorboat. Duncan drove down it as Addy wept, and Mark continued to rub her shoulders from behind. They came to a break in the trees. Out in the pasture the horses were grazing their way through another day. A few of them raised their heads in lazy recognition of the van coming down the driveway, though none made a move to approach it. Then suddenly Bruce came charging out from the back of the herd, galloping as hard and fast as a donkey could possibly go. His ears were slicked back along his neck and his muzzle was thrust forward like a racehorse. Clods of earth and sod flew in the air around him, and the horses that stood before him made way. Addy rolled down the window, spinning the crank with her good hand, and shouted out to him in the field as he ran. "Bruce!" she called. "There's my boy!" And he kept on running, flying for the farmhouse with all his heart so he could meet them there.

TIM GRIFFITH is originally from Southeastern Massachusetts but has spent the past decade and a half in the West. His stories have appeared in Santa Monica Review, Chicago Quarterly Review, Bellevue Literary Review, Tin House, Gettysburg Review, *and elsewhere. He teaches writing at Boise State University and is at work on a novel.*

Open Enrollment

Danielle Claro

Alice had not been keen on any of the death packages till now. Most were precious and corny, with their "memory mason jars" and cremains sachets. The most popular option, if you were to believe the marketing materials, included a reading of the will in the library of a historic home: *"Guests can help themselves to vintage props: pillbox hats, monocles, hand-carved pipes..."* No, thank you.

This one was different. This one felt like George. The branding wasn't gimmicky (no "Death 2.0" or "50 Ways to Leave Your Body"). It was direct, clean: "Last List: A Simple Plan for the End of Life." Pricing wasn't revealed till the end of the application—that's how they get you, George would say—but this was certainly on the modest end.

George had been uncharacteristically enthusiastic about the new healthcare bill. The best part—the 78.6 savings account, named for the average U.S. life expectancy—had gotten a lot of coverage. It would make end-of-life easier for working families, taking Big Death out of the equation, or so they said. Alice suspected a catch and yelled questions at NPR while she did the dishes.

She scanned the complete list of options once more—all the media companies were in on the action, plus the freshly pivoted pharma giants. Now Netflix had a death plan. Restoration Hardware.

Oprah, of course. Last month, one of the kids—was it Lizzie?—had sent a link for the *New York Review of Books* plan; it included Last Literary Rites. George would love that. But financially it wasn't possible. Alice sighed.

"More tea?" George had never said anything so small and tender. Without looking up, Alice smiled and nodded. George filled her cup. It took forever.

Alice didn't bother checking the balance of the 78.6 account. She didn't need to. It was in her head, like all their numbers. They had saved what they could—always managed to get the full match from the school. Only three percent, but still. They hadn't left money on the table, as Larry would have said…probably pounding an actual table as he said it.

Thirty-five years George had taught those eighth-graders. Some seventh too. The toughest age, everyone said, but George loved his kids. He loved their combativeness and the dare in their eyes. He loved to debate them and lose—that meant they were thinking. He had loved their confidence, unearned, something maybe he wished he'd had at their age, or ever. He loved to scare them with his outrageous (and fake) syllabus on the first day of each school year, win their respect or their fear or their ire. It was all valuable. All currency. He even reveled in the nasty reviews after Lizzie had shown him that awful web site. Why did she do that?

"George, honey, do you want a cherry tree or a pear tree?"

George peered over his glasses and flattened both hands on the newspaper. Those eyes, still so blue. Long pause. Always a long pause.

"I meant it when I said I want *you* to decide, Alice." He was sweet and stern, like he might be with one of his less resistant students. "That's my birthday present." He dropped back into his reading.

Alice would give George his actual gift at midnight, with a bowl of blueberries they'd share in bed. They would turn the clock back and make it 11:00. The year they met, daylight savings had also fallen on George's birthday. More time.

Like always, Alice had purchased George's gift months ahead. In March, she could find good cashmere at seventy-five percent off. She'd hide it away till October. It was a long, gratifying game, and the only thing she could think to reveal when, at book club, the topic had turned to secrets kept from spouses. Her friends—neighbors really—had laughed. This was all she could come up with?

George remarked every time he wore one of these cashmere gifts—a scarf, gloves, socks. "*Feel this, Alice. It's exceptionally soft, wouldn't you say?*" Gentle observation was out of character for George. At least for Old George, the George she had married. So these moments made Alice smile. But now all of life was cashmere. New George, whose heart was open to sparrows at the bird feeder, distant church bells, and the smell of an ordinary tomato, ran a quiet commentary of tender appreciation. It was like the crawl at the bottom of the screen on CNN.

Alice missed being the sunny one, the one who brought the beauty. She missed George's edge. She wanted to hear George curse when he banged his shin on the coffee table. She wanted to call out from the kitchen, "What happened, dear?" She wanted him to be too riled to respond.

"Pear tree, then," Alice said. "White flowers with a yellow center."

"Be sure to take everything that's included," George said. "If you don't opt in, they don't give it to you."

George sat tall in his chair and stretched his arms wide, revealing the front of his sweatshirt: *Chronic Malcontent*, it read, in velvety collegiate letters. A Father's Day gift at least a decade old.

Alice wanted to deliver some good news. The Farewell Trip section of the application was hopeful, so she read excerpts aloud: "They'll carry you into the sea on a lounge chair...if you can't walk. They'll set you down with the water lapping up around your feet and stay nearby to bring you back..."

"What's that?" George's voice was achingly curious. Alice wished he'd been too caught up in his article to reply. She opted to ignore him. Anyway, this next part was not something to share.

CASKET. Why does *casket* come *after* tree? So manipulative. Alice poked around for pricing, but this form was consistent:

None of the costs were revealed till you made all your selections; your account balance was applied against the total, then you were presented with a copay.

Alice suspected the shroud would represent considerable savings. But the only thing George had ever mentioned was some sort of casket. "A pine box," he'd said. Had he been kidding? Alice had looked for clues of what he truly wanted, but all he wanted was to live, to teach another ten years, to retire. To play with grandkids that didn't exist yet. To learn the banjo.

Alice clicked SHROUD. They had once talked about a green burial. Did George remember? She had to get through the form. It was the last day of open enrollment. How had she left this so long? Were there people everywhere filling out this application right now? That was comforting—the notion of company in this task. It should be a holiday, New Year's Eve in reverse; looking toward an ending, instead of a beginning.

The newspaper crinkled.

"Larry's son called," George said. "I meant to tell you."

"Oh? Which one?"

"Eric. He wants to come by," George said.

"I'll make lasagna," Alice said. "Or stew."

Larry and George had started together at the middle school, both in the history department. But after two years and one baby, Larry left for a training program at Grayson Brothers. He was a partner twelve years later, and had just begun considering retirement when he got the diagnosis.

His death had been very hard on George. How could it not be? They had talked every day for nearly thirty years. The package had helped; mainly it had benefited the family, but it eased the pain for George too. A big party at that nice French restaurant near the river, plus one-on-one catered visits. The family trip to St. John. Home hospice and morphine. Hospital beds upstairs and down, the chairlift. A fully doula'd death. Then burial at sea (Larry had been a Navy man). What most impressed Alice was the aftercare: creative therapy for the grandkids, with that lovely young woman. Was her name Elise? She helped them make a little play-shrine in the den with Larry's collection of ceramic turtles. A low cabinet, with smiling photos on the inside door, Larry's hats and ties for dress-up. Even his pipes. Alice was surprised that Eric allowed that, play-smoking, but people are different in grief.

Louise, Larry's wife, was still in therapy—the plan covered five years' worth, transitioning from bereavement to analysis to life building. It was hard not to be jealous, but that's what happens when you work in finance rather than in education. It should be the other way around.

Right there on Alice's screen were all Larry's benefits—the platinum option in each section. Here was the "non-ambulance transport from hospital to home hospice." Here was the "compassionate closet cleanout," a two-week affair with a spiritual organizer who guided the family through separating from each item.

Alice didn't dare hover her cursor near them. Some remnant of faith from childhood had her believing that if she was reasonable, not greedy, if she showed humility in filling out this form—her selections would be approved without a big copayment. Maybe the 78.6 account really did work. Maybe NPR was right.

Alice unchecked the box to autosend an email notification to the kids with the pre-filled subject line "Dad's farewell trip." She'd need to talk to them herself. They were so busy.

She sighed, then wished she hadn't. So many of the offerings at the Copper level were meaningless, off point, sideways to what you'd want. You should be able to trade in a religious service for a jazz trio and swap junky funeral favors for a book of poems. But she didn't want to burden George with her complaints.

George lifted his head from the paper, cleared his throat.

"I saw the New Partner form about halfway down," he said in his classroom voice, probably louder than he realized. "You should fill that out."

Alice shook her head.

"I'm not doing that," she said. She looked at George, who had already lowered his eyes.

"You can only access it during open enrollment," George said. He pretended to re-engage with an article.

"Well, that's terrible," Alice said.

"Be that as it may…" George rustled his paper.

Alice scrolled to the New Partner form. It linked out to a site called Till Death Do Us Part, owned by Tinder. Required, it said. She hunted for a work-around.

George drummed his pencil, thank God. He was doing the crossword puzzle. The rhythm broke the seal on their last exchange, and Alice's brain loosened enough to spot what she needed. There, buried in a dense block of text, was a barely tinted link that enabled her to bypass the New Partner section "for religious reasons." Click.

Buoyed by this small victory, Alice took a break. In the kitchen, she warmed the oven for the chicken, then climbed the step stool and pulled a jar from the top cabinet. The gummies were supposed to be for George. He stored them out of reach "just in case." In case what? Alice popped one in her mouth—a whole instead of a half—and sucked till there was a sweet-bitter drip in her throat. She started a pot of rice.

On the other side of the kitchen window, a pale brown cardinal—a female—pecked at the rose of Sharon buds. Why were there buds in October? Why was she even trying? She was getting nothing. They were too tight and too firmly attached. The branch wobbled. The bird hung on.

When the oven dinged, Alice slid the chicken onto the top rack. She let the warmth surround her face. Her necklace caught the heat, like it did every night.

The first day in their first-ever apartment, the pilot light had gone out. Alice hadn't thought to turn off the gas while she looked for matches. It was only a minute. But that was enough. The explosion singed her bangs and took some eyelashes. She and George screamed, then laughed. They were too young to appreciate how close they'd come to tragedy.

Now Alice lowered the flame under the rice and returned to her seat in the dining room. George was noiseless. The puzzle was done. He was in the Arts section. Alice touched a key, and the laptop came to life.

AFTERCARE, it shouted. The recommended option included one hour's worth of virtual sorting, followed by donation pickup.

What good would an hour do? "Boxes and bins must be sealed and on the first floor of the abode in advance of pickup." The screen asked what time Alice would want the donation truck. How should she know? She chose 3:00pm.

An ad popped up for a book: *Swedish Death Cleaning: How to Free Yourself from a Lifetime of Clutter*. Alice hit buy now.

"This tea is so good," George said, throwing back the last sip. "What is it?"

"Regular stuff from the market."

Alice had nearly come to the end of the form. All that was left was to upload the health proxy and choose Final Meds. She clicked morphine, because oxy had such a bad reputation, and because she'd once had morphine herself. It was in the hospital after her C-section. She'd felt so itchy, but also felt so happy. She wanted that for George. That kind of happy. She clicked the box agreeing to turn in extra pills at the pharmacy. Right.

She hit the big blue SUBMIT button and exhaled.

Inside the buffering circle the green 78.6 logo rotated and pulsed. Alice's lungs stayed on empty.

Your selections are being processed.
Please do not hit submit again.
Processing can take up to three minutes.

The oven bell dinged.

"Don't touch this," Alice said and flew toward the kitchen.

"I wouldn't dream of it," George smiled.

In two minutes, Alice was back, dropping silverware into the center of the table and wiping her hands on her apron. She slipped silently into her seat, so as not to disturb or disrespect the screen.

The green logo continued to spin. Alice hovered and forced an inhale. She fixed her eyes on the center of the screen and promised not to blink. Another long minute passed. Or maybe just ten seconds. Then a message in large type:

CONGRATULATIONS,
YOUR SELECTIONS HAVE BEEN APPROVED!

She read the sentence over and over. Her jaw began to uncoil. Her shoulders softened. She mouthed the words. George was in the kitchen. So she said them out loud: "Congratulations, your selections have been approved."

Then just below in small gray type she saw it.

Click here to see your copayment.

Alice clicked, and the figure slowly made its way to her brain: $113,500. Another message:

Click here to see what you qualify for with $0 copayment, based on the current balance of your 78.6 account.

Sick from adrenaline and outrage, Alice put one cold palm on her forehead. She followed the prompt. Buffering, and then:

With your complete balance applied, you are entitled to:

The Foil Package: *two pills for hastening death; local overnight trip with motel accommodations, including one meal for four, not to exceed $25 per person; cremation (transport of body to crematorium not included); email notification sent to up to 100 people; one hour virtual organizing; one hour grief counseling; one hour legal services.*

No casket, no shroud even, no farewell party, no memorial service, no proper vacation, nothing for the kids. No pear tree.

George set two steaming plates on the table.

"Done?" he asked, folding his paper. He didn't wait for an answer. He shuffled back to the kitchen and returned with a pitcher of water, a bit too heavy for him now. Then he sat down, pulling his chair so close that the steam from the rice fogged up his glasses.

"This looks wonderful," he said as he wiped his lenses. George pointed to the laptop with his chin. "Get everything you wanted?"

He was already slicing into his chicken.

Alice considered the peace in not knowing. Not knowing about the death package, the cruel reviews on ratemyteacher.com, the illness even. How would it be to not know?

"All set," Alice said. She closed her computer, pushed it deliberately out of reach and dropped her napkin in her lap.

"Thank you for arranging it." George said. "You're so good at these things."

He raised a triangle of juicy meat on his fork as if toasting. A trail of steam escaped the cut side like a tiny campfire between them.

"Mmmm!" George's eyes closed in barely manageable bliss. Alice wished there was music. Or the sound of kids. She wished she was hungry.

"What did you do to this chicken, dear?" George asked. "It's delicious."

It was the same chicken as always. The same chicken she had made for thirty-two years. She wanted to say so. To have a regular, unprecious exchange. A little volley of normalcy. But she stayed in character.

"Secret recipe," she whispered.

George reached across the table and took Alice's hand. "Let's have it for my birthday every year," he said.

Alice squeezed George's trembling fingers. "Yes, let's," she said. They smiled conspiratorially and held on tight.

DANIELLE CLARO *is a writer of fiction and nonfiction whose work has appeared in* McSweeney's, The Lascaux Review, Real Simple, Domino, *and many other publications. She is co-author, with Dr. Frank Lipman, of the* New York Times *bestselling wellness book* The New Health Rules. *She lives in New York's Lower Hudson Valley.*

Walking to Camano

Clemintine Guirado

You probably heard about it on the news—the girl in Washington State found wandering naked except for a pair of socks and a paper crown. *Missing Fourteen-Year-Old Girl Found Disoriented on Deception Pass, Police Say.* The media loved the sound of the name of the bridge, and they used it over and over. It's technically two bridges on Route 20 connecting Whidbey and Fidalgo, with an islet in the middle. The water, an alchemical green, roils 180 feet below. Hundreds of people have jumped there and that's what the ranger thought she was doing.

The high school student had minor rope burns on her wrists and drugs in her blood—heavy opiates and dextromethorphan (the active ingredient in cold medicine). She told authorities she was abducted by an unknown and unseen attacker. Her horse—a buckskin quarter horse—escaped the pasture and she went out to catch him. She lured him with a handful of grain, got his halter on and was walking home when a white van with tinted glass pulled up. The kind of van she and her friends used to call an *abductomobile.* The girl stepped forward, thinking they wanted directions. She heard the side door of the van slide open, but before she could turn around, a pillowcase dropped over her head. Strong arms seized and dragged her in.

The buckskin was found running down Saratoga Road, trailing his lead behind him.

The girl was missing for three days.

She showed the police the place where she'd woken up tied to a tree. She showed them the rope and the pillowcase.

She didn't remember the three days.

They found her story suspicious. The pillowcase—a yellow daisy print—matched one from the girl's own home. Route 20 was only ten yards from the place where she was bound behind a thin veil of pines. There were candy wrappers everywhere and buried feces and toilet paper some distance from the tree.

The pharmacist at Rexall recalled the fourteen-year-old shoplifting the candy and a family-sized bottle of NyQuil. He ignored the theft. He felt sorry for her; everyone knew about what happened to her mom. The opiates in her system matched an empty box of Dilaudid suppositories prescribed to the girl's mother for pain in the latter stages of bone cancer.

Then a security video at the local hardware store showed the girl purchasing the rope and duct tape.

There was talk of legal action for a false kidnapping report, but she got off easy—no juvenile time, only a stint at Western State Psychiatric Hospital.

Everyone assumed she did it for attention—a boy (Tobin Sulky) had broken up with her. They figured the girl got her flair for the dramatic from her mother, who had recently committed suicide by jumping off the side of a Washington State ferry. Rescue boats and a helicopter crew from the Naval Air Station searched for the mother for four hours before they quit. They said nobody could have survived in the water, particularly an eighty-pound woman who was already dying.

The news didn't name the girl—she was a minor.

That girl was me.

*   *   *

Back on the island, I'm scared someone might recognize me, even though my hair is dyed "Moon Gold" and I'm seven years older. I hide inside my stepfather and step-stepmother's house and wear shades or hang my hair over my face on mandatory outings, slumped down in the car outside the Clinton Foodmart. Family never says anything directly about what happened—but you can see it in the tension of a shoulder or the flicker of an eyelid—you can hear it in a heavy pause. I'm like an apparently clean hotel room sprayed with luminol, just waiting for the black light to expose the messy splatters.

*   *   *

My stepdad, Carlos, reluctantly drives me to the ferry before dawn for my job interview. We're early and he parks on the little side road where people drop off and pick up their loved ones.

The truck fills with our usual miasma of tension and dread.

"You can go if you want," I say.

"I'll wait." He still holds the wheel like he's driving. A lifelong carpenter, he cut his thumb and two fingers off with a power saw a couple years ago. He held it above his head—a rookie move—leading some to theorize he did it on purpose, subconsciously. They sewed most of his hand back on, but he's still missing the tip of the middle finger.

After my mom died, Carlos was considered a very eligible bachelor. All the neighbors and my mom's friends hoped to replace her. Contenders acted motherly towards me until he got tired of them. Six months *before* she died, a reporter feigned interest in my terminally ill mother and pitched a "local artist" feature to the *Whidbey Record.* To get in the house and lay groundwork. That's the one he married.

Carlos clears his throat. "Where are you interviewing?"

In my bag I have a black wig and a pair of blue sequined stilettos for the audition. I don't know yet this isn't a practical kind of shoe for stripping—the sequins flake off like fish scales, leaving a bare patch.

"Thirteen Coins." This is the only restaurant I can think of this early in the morning.

Everyone was surprised when I got into Pacific Lutheran. My siblings (half and step) got college paid for, but I'm not considered a good risk. My real dad said, "I paid for tuition at Western State Psychiatric, you're welcome." So, I've been scraping up the money myself. I was recently fired as a baker at the crumpet shop in Pike Place Market. It involved a performance in front of a window, pouring batter into metal circles, theatrically flipping the rings onto a long metal spatula while tourists watched. I kept thinking I saw island people and abandoned the crumpets to burn while I hid in the bathroom. The *Nam myoho renge kyo* Buddhists that owned the place said they were sorry, but if I chanted, I would find another job. They were right. Less than a block down from the crumpet shop was the strumpet shop—and Jessie already worked there. The peepshow was called The Amusement Center back in the day, but now it's known as The Lusty Lady. It's women-run but Jessie says the women aren't nice.

"Thirteen Coins?" Carlos asks.

I realize my mistake; nobody my age waits table there—it's all old guys with sad pomades and wet gravel voices. Men who live in residential hotels and no longer even have heroin to keep them warm.

"The one downtown."

For someone who is pro-science and anti-mystic, Carlos can be very psychic. I attempt to distract him. "Did you know the Sound froze over once and people walked across to Camano Island?"

"That's impossible." His lip curls, like he's personally offended by how dumb I am. "It's saltwater."

A flower of anger unfurls inside my chest.

"I'll bet you twenty dollars," I say.

Carlos stretches out his scarred hand to shake.

Jessie and her mom pull up and climb out of a rusted Nissan. They both have the same long, wavy amber hair, big breasts, and big bones. Jessie has more meat. A self-identified Viking, she's dressed in what appears to be a bearskin cloak, green leggings, and tennis shoes she painted herself. She's in one of her moods—quietly crying and clenching her fists.

When we have put twenty yards between ourselves and her mom and my stepdad, we exhale audibly and burst into laughter.

"Do you find you regress when you're back on the island for more than two hours?" I say.

"Yes." Jessie wipes the side of her wrist across her eyes.

Across the water, the mainland looks like a black slug covered in jewels, the lights of Mukilteo glittering against its body. We wait at the dock with the walk-ons, breathing in the fishy diesel. I'm sure every car in line contains someone from high school. From my invisibility hoodie, I scan the faces of commuters in carpenter pants and office-drudge-wear.

I take out my phone and scour the internet for evidence of the frozen Sound, but there is nothing. Then I search for Deception Pass. *Girl fakes kidnapping* comes up before *Strait in Washington State*.

I know it's true but I can't remember where I learned this fact. It's like a red object under layers of ice—a dog's chew toy or an apple—where you can only see a hint of color, really far down.

Jessie's crying again. Usually I ignore her; nothing you say ever makes her feel better, but I'm scared she'll escalate and draw attention.

"So, when you're dancing, you can see the guys in the windows?" I ask.

"Some of the windows," she says. "Half have that glass they use on cop shows—like for a lineup."

"I don't know if I can look at them."

"You don't have to make eye contact, but management likes you to pretend. Just look at their foreheads or go blurry."

Cars line up behind the white line as the ferry churns in, black water swirling. It's the *Cathlamet*.

We are island girls and know each of the ferries—the *Issaquah*, the *Klickitat*, the little *Kulshan*. We know the layout, the video games, the vending machines, the art—on the *Olympic*, Jessie's mom currently has a tryptic of mixed-media, fabric fish floating behind Plexiglas. My mother was an artist too. My stepdad's new house is full of her paintings and his wife has told me, "It's hard to compete with a dead woman."

Ferry workers jump off before the metal lip bridges the gap. They're out in the elements all day in their orange smocks—back and forth—but they're union and make a ton of money so no one feels sorry for them.

I compulsively check their faces as they wind the thick-furred ropes around the cleats. The ferry guy with a red beard could be Tobin Sulky's older brother but he's not.

Jessie has accelerated to whispering *fuck, fuck, fuck* and kicking posts. I turn my hood and move a couple yards away. There is the moan of rigging and dock.

Since we were kids, she was too shy to speak in front of adults— my grandmother thought she was retarded—but when we were alone, she was wild and in charge. She smeared shit in the dryers at the laundromat and made crank calls while I knelt on the floor beside her, laughing into a cushion. "Is my mommy there?" she said in a convincing little girl voice. "She gave me this number to call if there was a 'mergency. She isn't home yet." And when they told her it was the wrong number and hung up, she would call them again and again. "Is my mommy there?"

These days she has a cable access show where she overshares and dances around in body paint. On the Solstice, she rides with naked cyclists through Seattle.

She's the only friend I retained after the incident.

The thin nylon cord that signals the walk-ons is flung to the ground and the three passengers from the other side surge forward like racehorses, feeling the pressure of the car engines starting behind them. When the last car is unloaded, Red Beard summons us and we file on, shoes clanking over the Braille of patterned metal.

Women enter the left staircase—it goes almost directly into the Ladies'. The men climb the right, to the Men's. Red Beard studies my face. Heart beating, I duck after Jessie's broad, fur-clad back. In my sessions at Western State, the shrink liked to use the phrase "delusions of reference." He said I was misperceiving irrelevant and innocuous phenomena as relating to me personally.

The stairs are built for giants. I'm aware the hole in my tights might be visible to the person climbing behind me and it makes me tense my thighs. I'm not what you'd call a natural for a peepshow. I've never been at ease dancing—I'm not loose and comfortable in my body. I was born with mild cerebral palsy and went through a series of surgeries and wore a brace when I was a kid. Now my C.P. is barely noticeable except when I jump rope, or when it's below freezing. Jessie coached me for a week, showing me how to undulate and how to lean forward and run my hands up and down my thighs.

There is a weighted metal door like a spaceship hatch. Jessie holds it open for me and I hold it for the woman behind me—that's the etiquette. In the restroom we put our makeup on with the others. Everyone has their straightening irons out and they look dead under the greenish fluorescent lights. I smear thick foundation over my freckles. I'm going for unrecognizable. I just dyed my hair, but my roots are already a trail of ants crawling in a line across my scalp. There is little chatter. Commuters are not happy people.

*   *   *

Three days before my fourteenth birthday, my mother, who was going to die soon, asked her sisters to take her to the mainland to buy gifts. Everyone thought she was much too delicate for that long of a trip, but my mother insisted, and they carried her to the car.

They took her around the Alderwood Mall in her wheelchair. They went to Nordstrom's, Penney's, and Crabtree and Evelyn. They said she had a good day, she seemed clearer and in less pain than she had been in weeks. On the ferry on the way back, she wanted to get out of the car and go upstairs for a hot chocolate. They helped her into her coat and into the chair and wheeled her to the elevator. Aunt Robin said that my mother was smiling, eyes bright. Her head was wrapped in a yellow scarf with a print of California poppies. They drank watery hot chocolate from the vending machine and sat watching the rain pelt the glass.

Then a girl who was playing a video game, suddenly dropped to the floor and had a grand mal seizure—eyes rolled back, flopping limbs akimbo, heels stuttering on the tile. Her brother began to force a wooden spoon in her mouth that he apparently kept on his person.

"Make him stop," my mother said.

"She could choke on that," Robin said. "People don't do that anymore."

"Why don't you mind your own business?"

"Use your wallet, something soft. She could break her teeth," Robin said.

"We always use this spoon, bitch."

"Don't you call me that."

Onlookers collected around my aunt, the angry boy, and the thrashing girl. Urine darkened her jeans.

The first mate arrived and took over from the boy; the girl eventually stopped seizing and apologized shamefacedly for all the fuss, and my aunts returned to the table.

My mother's wheelchair was gone.

They looked for her in this bathroom, the snack bar, and the other side of the ferry, but she wasn't in any of those places. Eventually they found the chair and her orange and yellow scarf outside on the observation deck by the rail.

It's a big boat, the *Cathlamet*, and they searched it some more, going downstairs to make sure she hadn't managed to get to back in the car. They stopped the boat, though no one really believed yet that my mother had jumped.

One of my fantasies, when I was younger and sometimes still, was that my mother had not climbed over the side of a ferry and drowned, but had instead slipped into a stranger's car on the lower deck—a stranger who happened to be a scientist possessing a vaccine that cured cancer (I imagined a blue vial of serum in a fitted velvet case) and they ran away to a new life on the other side of the world. Over the years, I embellished my vision. I recently learned of a hotel constructed entirely of ice. I think it was in Sweden, but I liked the idea of Norway better. I saw my mother living there in that translucent palace, tucked under reindeer skins with her lover, breath steaming.

*   *   *

Me and Jessie know the exact shift in sound the engine makes when the boat nears the other side. It's uncool to go downstairs too early. Only tourists do that.

We sleep on the bus and wake up gritty eyed at the Park and Ride. Out past the porta-potty and the freeway, there's a field. Above the field, a swan flies by.

"Look," I tell Jessie, but it's gone when she raises her head from her phone.

I have the feeling of being observed—a little prickle at the back of the neck. I scan the people waiting to transfer. A fifty-year-old woman in a Catholic girl skirt and goth eyeliner, a young man in an itchy ankle monitor, a grossly pregnant teen, a person on crutches with five-o'clock shadow, wearing all pink with a pink cast-bootie.

*   *   *

Downtown, we walk past the store where I bought my wig. A row of eyeless heads mutely observe us from shallow, velvet depressions. We pass Burger King and Déjà Vu where a sign reads: *Fifty beautiful girls and one ugly one.* Then, Pike Place Market—giant clock, pink fish on ice, cute boys hawking vegetables and flowers. The fish guys toss a big silver salmon back and forth shouting for the tourists. We stop in the crumpet shop to get my last check and they give us free crumpets with raspberry jam.

*   *   *

Inside The Lusty Lady it smells of bleach-mop and semen. One of the janitors, a young skinny guy with hunched shoulders, escorts us to the dressing room and waits while we're buzzed in. Outside there is a camera and inside, a video monitor so you can tell who is at the door. I wish I had a set up like that everywhere I go.

One naked woman with an elegant bob sits on a piece of paper towel on a chrome stool at the mirror, another girl with a very large, pale bottom is bent over spraying Windex. They turn to greet us with exuberant cheer. Jessie is shy with them. "This is my friend," she says.

"I'm Velveeta," the one with the Windex says. "Welcome."

The bobbed one tells me she's called Ginger but is changing her name to Ice. She wears long satin gloves and one of her front teeth doesn't match. My mother had a dead tooth too, she got it horsing around with her sisters—a fall onto cement.

The manager, a cosmetic redhead in vintage pedal pushers and jeweled, horn-rimmed glasses, explains the rules. Lotion or oil isn't allowed—it could smudge the glass and the mirrors. Only one dancer is permitted to wear black at a time. You can get fired for weight fluctuation. Jessie has been warned. Costumes must show nipples and vagina at all times. It isn't stripping; you're already stripped.

I initial number seven: *Absolutely no datemaking or anything remotely resembling datemaking!! This is extremely serious and could have this theater closed down in a heartbeat!! You will never know if your customer is a plainclothes police officer or not. This theater isn't interested in breaking the law.*

I keep thinking, *I'm not really going to do this,* as I peel off my jeans and fold them.

The "music box" is mirrored and filled with a pink, flattering light. I wait in the wings, naked in my wig and blue shoes. I watch five pink women dance in slow motion. The one with blue hair rotates out and after a little push from Velveeta, I rotate in.

Through the speakers, the Zombies croon "The Time of the Season." Screens slide up and down with the clunk of tokens and a faint whirr. Jessie told me you can tell which window the manager lady is behind—it'll be one of the mirrored ones and will stay open because they loaded it with tokens. I get in front of that one and smile with weird enthusiasm. Once I start dancing, it's totally fine. I have a raspberry seed in my teeth, but I'm not scared anymore.

They hire me at a buck more an hour than they normally start girls out. Because of my good attitude.

*   *   *

"You look like a raccoon." Carlos kneads a ball of yeasty dough on the butcher block counter. Above him hangs one of my mother's paintings—a giant O'Keeffe-like vagina-flower in reds and purples.

I didn't bother taking my stage makeup off. I thought it had blurred to a respectable level.

I stand at the sink, listening to a lost gray whale in the sound. You can hear it breathing all the way from inside the kitchen, a quarter mile from the beach—a distant, regular swoosh, unbelievably clear and loud like some aquatic obscene phone-caller. Everyone has been down to see it but me.

"I don't know why you bothered." My step-stepsister wiggles her hand in front of my face. Her black hair is shiny, like ironed ribbon. "It's not like you're coming with us." There's a play after dinner at the Clyde Theater. The thought of entering the Clyde makes me shiver—it's not like an AMC where you can get lost in the dark—before a movie or play, everyone in town stands up and yaks loudly, like they're at a reunion.

"I had a job interview."

"At a kabuki theater?" she says.

I can hear the sliding-glass doors open and close. Through the window above the sink, the others move through the nighttime garden in the fluorescent spotlight from the deck.

At the edge of the pasture, past the bluff, a full moon shines high above Camano Island.

"*Are* you coming?" Carlos says. "You can't hide in here forever."

I look at him. "I need to go to bed early. I got that job."

His posture is stiff and careful. "At Thirteen Coins?"

I nod.

"In five minutes, punch this down." Carlos nods to the dough he's covered with a clean dish cloth. He wipes his hands on a towel and picks up a metal colander. I look at the nub of his middle finger. I'm not the only one who makes mistakes.

*   *   *

Everyone said I kidnapped myself; that I was a liar. After they showed me the evidence—the surreal black and white videotape where I stood at the Ace Hardware counter—I had to accept the former, but I never lied. I saw the white van clear as day, sucked air through cloth, heard gravel ping as we drove away.

An outcast before the incident—a bookish girl with an orthopedic shoe—I was despised afterward. The crown detail got around—the kids called me Princess McNuggets, though the crown was from Burger King. Denis Demartini said, "Princess, you want to show me your jewels?"

I had to move to Alaska, and I changed my name to Mia.

I have no memory of buying the rope or the cough medicine and while I did, on occasion, take my mother's leftover pain-meds—to numb out my wretched teenage existence—I didn't on the day I disappeared. I know for a fact I used all but two of the waxen bullets in their silver foil several months earlier. Concerned about becoming a drug addict, I tossed the last two suppositories in the trash, then later changed my mind and fished them out. They ended up melting out of their foil into my coat pocket before I could insert them. I tried licking the opiate-laced gunk and scraping it off the fabric with my teeth, to no avail—it had soaked into the cotton and I wasn't so desperate I would eat my pocket. The withdrawals were unpleasant but relatively mild.

As for the cough syrup, I wasn't an idiot. What sort of moron would ingest a crippling amount of over-the-counter NyQuil? What would be the point? If I were going to fake my own kidnapping, I would have *committed*. I would have beaten myself bloody, I would have burned satanic messages into my abdomen, I would have shit all over myself. What kind of despicable amateur would stage a plan so lame?

*   *   *

Out the window, I watch everyone gathering vegetables and the dahlias Carlos has grown in all his gardens. My step-stepmother fills a colander with radishes, raven hair shining a diamond crown of light from the porchlight. An evil queen.

What must it be like to be them—to have always been wanted, all your life?

The years after my mother died were a gray, drippy blur. I can't remember in what order I stayed with whom. I lived in a sort of fugue state, crashing with family members and friends of family, in their dens and sewing rooms, leaving a wake of unpleasantness and betrayal behind me. My mother's friend Aurora in Victoria told me that I was "bristly" and in Spokane, I overheard my aunt Sidney say, "Sofia wears out her welcome everywhere she goes." I even lived with my real dad for a couple months in an ancient canvas army tent in his back yard. "Try not to pee in the same spot twice," he told me. "It ruins the grass."

I punch down the dough like collapsed silk.

*   *   *

At The Lusty Lady, everyone's Polaroids are displayed on the wall next to the cashier's counter. In mine, I have my kabuki mask of make-up on, the Cleopatra wig and Cherries-in-the-Snow lipstick, a color that will later be discontinued. Jessie and I spent hours deliberating on our stage names. Jessie goes by Jade, and I go by Lil' Egypt. This makes more sense when I wear the wig but less when I don't. It's from the song, "Lil' Egypt does the hoochie coochie singing yiiiiiiinnnnnnnnnn' yang," but nobody gets that reference. "You'll make more money with your real hair," the girls say. "Blondes make the most money." They're correct, but I'm still an innocent playing dress-up.

Shifts are four hours with ten-minute breaks once an hour. We do double shifts. The regulars ignore the beat, but I'm a novice, so I quickly tire myself out. Jessie cradles her large breasts in her arms like twin infants and wears a pair of green tights with the crotch and part of the thighs cut out to form a type of chaps. She has a spacey, unfocused gaze and moves slowly like a marsh reed, hair hanging in Titian ripples. Velveeta spends most of her time down on all fours on the carpet, resting on her elbows with her face on her hands, quivering her big butt just a little, just enough not to get fired.

I like to watch the graceful Ginger-Ice, who is a real dancer and wears fleshy-beige jazz shoes. She has a patch of sliver-thin scars on her abdomen. A lot of the girls have them and Jessie and I puzzle over it for a while. Apparently, they're razor scars from some kind of S&M sex currently popular in a crowd we don't circulate in.

I feel exempt from being recognized in the glowing pink room. The floor we dance on is higher than the floor of the customer's booths, so we look cozily down on them like zoo animals. Some jerk, some pull, some crane their eyes past us to eyeball another girl in the reflection on the walls. It turns out I don't mind eye contact or any of what I thought I'd mind.

*   *   *

The boy strokes himself delicately with just the tips of his fingers. He plays a little game with himself, doling out his tokens one at a time, hoping he will finish and still have coins jingling in his pocket for tomorrow. The screen slides almost all the way down and he crouches, turning his head to the side and follows it, his nose in the crack like a ferret and just when I think, *He's finally run out*, he pushes in another token at the last minute and the screen whirs back up.

I turn around and bend over to rest. I have heard the other girls say, "I'm going to let my vagina look at you now."

I have abandoned the wig and my hair hangs down, almost sweeping the floor, and the blood runs to my forehead. I can see the other dancers through my hair; I can see myself in the mirrored wall; I now know my face and body from every angle. Upside down I'm a totally different person. But it gets boring fast. For the first couple days, I entertained myself changing into different costumes during breaks, but soon it became tedious. My feet hurt. Jessie says you can just show up naked with no make-up or heels, but you won't get any raises if you do that.

*   *   *

In Mukilteo, we wait in the shelter across from Ivar's in the dark. Wind whips our clothes.

I feel eyes on my neck. There are silhouettes of fishermen on the dock. A flashlight beam sweeps the gray planks, illuminates tackle and a bucket. A woman in a jean jacket squats over a pile of baby dogfish. She meets my gaze and grimaces. The light trembles and swings up and I see a man with long scraggly black hair like one of those witch wigs you can buy at the drugstore on Halloween. He is staring right at me and Jessie. The beam is switched off and he disappears.

"Do you see those people looking at us?"

"No," Jessie said. "Where?"

"Over there."

"All I see is the fishermen."

Jessie's hair slashes in the wind, blowing into my mouth.

*   *   *

At my mother's memorial, we had no ashes; we tossed flowers into the sound. Carlos stood with his jeans rolled up, the edges getting wet, and the wind blew petals back in his face. All the orange and yellow dahlias washed back onto the beach. I felt self-conscious, like people were looking at me to see if I would cry. Many awkward people were there. Tobin Sulky. My future step-stepmother. I didn't like the way my mother's friend Aurora was keening, so I stood back near the beach path and picked and ate berries—pink salmonberries and orange thimbleberries. The salmonberries smelled like sex and tasted bitter and fishy, and the thimbleberries were sour, but I kept eating them until it was time for Aunt Robin to play guitar.

*   *   *

Again, I feel the current of attention. I glance toward the brightly lit windows of Ivar's, the people dining, the white tablecloths, the fishing nets on the walls, the busboys carrying gray plastic tubs. A couple eating a pile of red crabs are looking intently out the window in my direction, their faces greasy with butter. The man takes a pull on his Coke. The woman raises a crab leg and gives me a sinister smile and wink. I hope I don't have to go back to the hospital.

*   *   *

Jessie's mom drops me off. Everyone is asleep in the house. I figure it's safe to go down to see the whale, who has been stranded all week.

Across the water, there is a house lit up over on Camano. The small grey whale paces back and forth, bumping the buoy attached to someone's crab pot. Its sonic breath is so loud that I don't hear the man until he's right beside me.

"Hey," he says in the gentle, apologetic way of a guy trying not to come off as a rapist on a dark beach.

It has been many years, but I recognize his voice immediately— it's Shane Osborne, the older brother of Jessie's best friend Megan. Megan and Shane grew up in a house missing crucial walls. Their hippie-psychologist parents designed it with a big open space in the middle—there were dividers between the bedrooms, but you could see into the loft from the downstairs living area and of course you could hear everything.

"I didn't know you were back in town," I say.

"Me neither—I mean, that you were." He has a sweet face with a thin nose and a prematurely receding hairline.

I'm not embarrassed because Shane has more reasons than me to not want to be seen. After high school, he dropped out of college and joined the Moonies and more recently he was living in his van and got mistakenly arrested as a sex offender (early morning piss; school zone).

I ask about the cult thing, and he tells me he was wandering around San Francisco when these pretty hippie girls told him, "You look lost." They invited him to the Napa Valley to hangout and sing around the fire. Everyone was extra-friendly and clapped hard when he played guitar.

"What kind of stuff did you guys sing?"

"'If I Had a Hammer,' stuff like that." Shane shrugs. "Next thing I knew, I was selling lithographs door to door in Oakland in the snow."

When the tide comes in, the whale swims in very close, as if it has only been waiting for the beach to disappear. It swims in urgent circles, palpably trying to communicate.

"You need to catch up with the others," Shane says. "They've gone to Mexico."

We sing the whale some of the songs Shane knew from Moonie summer camp until the water laps our shoes.

* * *

Me and Jessie do a shift of "double-trouble." The Private Pleasures booth is tiny—we can't stand up. We make a nest of pillows and quilts on the platform. In the music box, we tower above the men, but here, the man looms. This changes the dynamic unpleasantly.

There is a display window to the hall and a microphone we're supposed to lure people in with, but we're too shy—we just wait. I tell her I saw Shane. She says Megan is married now. She lives on a remote San Juan island where she and her husband are the only people.

When a man enters the customer door, we close the gold curtain. I watch to see the denomination of bills inserted in the slot so I can set the meter. I perform a stylized self-fondle while Jessie does the same. Neither of us use this method in real life. I'm a defiler of pillows and Jessie has a complicated thigh-squeezing technique.

We only pick up the phone if they make us. We're still too young and dumb to know we should negotiate an additional tip. Jessie is no help, morose, sprawled like a beached Mermaid.

A foot fetishist comes in and explains he likes foot sex, slow, with lots of toe action. We accommodate this, Jessie's sturdy Viking leg and my freckled limb, soles embracing. The customer doesn't seem to mind us laughing. He just tells us, "Slower."

* * *

On Tuesday, a beautiful man enters the Private Pleasures booth. Early forties, haunted green eyes, a swoop of dark hair damp from shower or rain—the face of an English actor who specializes in miniseries with wellsprings of desire and impediments to love. Sexy tormented priests. Doves bursting from parapets. He wears a milky fishermen's sweater.

I nudge Jessie. He's exactly her type—girlish and old. Her eyes flick over him then glaze over in some private misery. He winks at her, then pulls off his sweater. Underneath he wears a Monterey Jazz Festival T-shirt. He ties the nice sweater around his waist. I worry he'll ejaculate on the sleeves.

He points to Jessie and then the phone. She picks it up like it's a turd.

I can hear him say, "I want you to tell me a story."

"No," Jessie says.

I snatch the receiver. "Hi! Would you like a show?"

"I'd love to see you sixty-nine each other." His voice is creamy, modulated. Naturally, the customers want this, but technically it's illegal. We've been told you can simulate cunnilingus by moving your head around while your hair screens the lack of authenticity.

We clamber into an ungainly position, lumbering giantesses in a glass box. It's embarrassing. I'm on top with my face close to Jessie's vagina, breathing in the specific smell she's had since we were children—sweet-sour washcloth, her unique chemical stew. She doesn't like to shave, so she bleaches her pubes. I swirl my hair around, but the customer doesn't buy it. He raps on the glass and I pick up the phone.

"You aren't doing anything," he says.

"We don't want to," I say, "We're just friends."

"Your friend doesn't look very happy." He works his penis in his fist.

I glance at Jessie, flat on her back crying again. I have a professional work ethic.

"She's moody." I cover the receiver with my hand. "Jade, why don't you go take a break."

"Okay." Jessie ties her kimono and clumsily crawls off the platform.

The man buttons himself, but he still holds the phone. He regards me with an intense, complicated expression—like he's just recognized me.

"I know you," he says. "You're Daisy."

I shake my head. "Lil' Egypt."

"Daisy girl." His voice sounds crazy and sing-song. "I know what really happened."

In the brightly lit box, I feel like Alice swollen too big for the rabbit's house.

"What you mean?"

"I know the guy who did it," he says. "He told me he made you buy the rope."

A wintry current runs the length of my spine and my arm-hairs bush out.

"I would remember that."

"He threatened you and he gave you a drug to forget."

"What kind of drug?"

"The kind surgeons use so that you won't remember all the terrible things they did."

*   *   *

When I freed myself from the bag on my head, I felt comforted by the faded daisies. I was still too drugged to understand those flowers spelled trouble for me. I didn't even feel the crown. My mother bought the set of yellow sheets at the St. Vincent de Paul. We had a dinghy and a crab pot then. Carlos threw the females and babies back and brought home the males in the wiggling daisy pillowcases. My mother dropped them alive into boiling water; they made a shrieking hiss before their shells turned red and they quit struggling. I protested.

She bent over the pot, smiling, her hennaed curls catching the steam. "It's over quick."

*   *   *

"What about the pillow case?" I ask.

"My friend said he went in your house and watched you when you were sleeping."

A broken, juddering filmstrip unspools behind my eyes.
Figures walk across a sea of ice.
The green-eyed man presses a Coke can to my lips.
A crow explodes off a branch in a cloud of green dust. "It's pollen," he says. "That's how pine trees mate."

*   *   *

He pushes his large, spatulate hand against the window. I can tell he wants me to put my palm up to his like a wife in a prison movie. I press my left hand to the glass and with my right, I slap the panic button.

"You don't have a friend," I say.

By the time I open the door, he's gone. I know I should be scared or sad or angry, but there is something else—I'm pleased.

*   *   *

They shut the club down while police take fingerprints and go through the security camera. A policewoman with a French braid escorts me and Jessie to a patrol car. I imagine it will be like before—they will interrogate me like a criminal while I flip through their yearbook of rapists and murderers.

Outside it has rained and the sidewalks are wet, reflecting the pink lights of the Lusty. The metal shutters of the vegetable stands are pulled shut and Pike Place Market is empty. A mild wind blows an empty cup across the cobblestones. The giant red neon clock radiates against the dark sky.

Jessie abruptly stops, her fur cloak rippling around her calves. "I have to tell you something."

Me and the policewoman wait. There is the smell of fish and flowers. I've forgotten my coat, by I don't care.

"I know that guy," Jessie says. "He used to teach tennis at the same club as my dad."

*   *   *

At the station, they drape silver Mylar around my shoulders and take Jessie to a different room.

"What is this for?" I flap the crinkly foil. I feel festive.

"To keep you warm," the cop with the braid says.

"I don't have hypothermia."

"It's for shock."

"I feel great." I am shaky but light. I remember that it was my mom who told me about the sound freezing over.

Officer Sheila DenOtter grew up on the island too—on the other side—in Oak Harbor by the military base. She gives me a Snickers bar from her desk and helps me find the old *Whidbey Record* article. The headline reads: *Walking to Camano.* In the 1930s there was an influx of fresh water from a series of heavy rainstorms, then temperatures below freezing for over a week.

"I'm going to win twenty dollars," I say.

*   *   *

Me and Jessie fall asleep in the squad car on the way to Mukilteo, her cloak covering us like a bearskin blanket. They are going to drive us all the way to the other side. We wait in the ferry line in front of Ivar's. Officer Sheila cracks the window. There is the weary clanking of the metal stanchions being dragged across the boat's lip. A woman beckons in her glowing orange vest and a stream of headlights flow up the hill toward Everett. As the last two cars disembark, the walk-ons surge forward and press impatiently against the gate.

CLEMINTINE GUIRADO writes and teaches in Nashville, Tennessee. She was a Wallace Stegner Fiction Fellow at Stanford University and a Carl Djerassi Fiction Fellow at the University of Wisconsin. She is currently finishing a novel called The Universal Detectives, *of which "Walking to Camano" is a chapter.*

The Tree That Stood Alone in the Desert

David DeGusta

Niamey, Niger, 1972

Issam was about to leave his office for lunch when the boy brought the letter to him. The Libyan stamps told him it was from home and he recognized Maram's handwriting, the tiny curls of her Arabic beautiful but nearly indecipherable. He read the letter and the anger in her words went straight to his stomach. Tea, he would go drink tea at the old woman's house. That would help. Nobody talked to him there, he could think. Issam folded the letter from his wife and slid it into the back pocket of his jeans.

The men lay on rugs in the shade of an acacia tree in the courtyard of the old woman's house. They wore dark robes, blues and greens, with gauzy white scarves around their heads. Small glasses of tea left circles in the dirt. A dented metal pot rested by a plastic serving tray loaded with empty glasses. Issam took a maroon rug from a dusty stack by the pot and joined the men in the shade, a brown Libyan among black Nigeriens. He sipped his tea and fought the urge to look again at the letter.

A boy ran into the yard and the men looked up.

"Issam?" asked the boy.

Issam nodded.

"The telephone," said the boy, and ran off.

Issam raised himself off his rug. It wouldn't be Maram calling. She had been clear in her letter that the decision was his: Give up his job in Niamey and come back to Tripoli and be a proper husband, or else she would find a new one. He walked down the dirt road to his office, a cement building with faded yellow paint and a tin roof. A small wooden addition leaned against it and served as his bedroom when he was in Niamey. He had been here for five months this time. Most days the heat drove him out of the office by noon. Someone would get him if anything important happened.

He sat on the office desk, the wood cool under him, and picked up the phone, black plastic warm in his hand.

"Issam here."

"It's Tarek," came the voice, scratchy and echoing. "I am in Agadez. There is a problem."

Issam picked up a pencil, then tossed it aside and reached for a pen.

"Lotfi," said Tarek. "He hit a tree."

Issam thought to ask how they came to hit a tree in a desert, but it didn't matter. It had happened. "How is the truck?"

"Fine. Just the bumper, but I can fix that."

"And the cargo?"

"The beams and poles are fine."

"So what is the problem?"

"The people are telling us it is a special tree," said Tarek.

"When Lotfi hit the tree, he made it special." With three trucks crisscrossing the Sahara there were bound to be problems. The goat you hit was always the owner's prized goat, valuable beyond reckoning. He expected such problems, but he also expected his drivers to handle them. It was as much a part of driving as shifting gears.

"I think it was already a special tree," said Tarek. "It was by itself. Alone. The one alone in the desert."

"The one by the track? Next to the well? That is three hours from Agadez."

"I got a ride here. To call you. Some Tuaregs are using the well. They do not permit the truck to leave."

Issam grimaced at the mention of Tuaregs. Last month a Frenchman on a motorcycle spooked some Tuareg camels and got his throat slit. They did that to a Frenchman.

"You need me to come," said Issam.

"The Tuaregs want compensation for the tree."

"Will the cargo, the metal, be safe with just Lotfi?" He trusted Tarek. Of the half dozen drivers, he was the most reliable and easygoing.

"I have a ride back," said Tarek. "I will be with Lotfi tonight."

"I will leave tomorrow morning and be there by the night."

Issam hung up. Maybe better to not tell Salah, not yet. His cousin owned their little trucking company, but his stomach couldn't take an argument, not after Maram's letter. He was the manager and he would make sure they still turned a profit on this load, Tuareg trouble or not.

Trucks going through Agadez left early in the morning. Tomorrow he would find a place in one. If he knew the driver he would get a seat in the cab, otherwise he would be in back. He would need to bring someone with him of course. Usually, he took a government official to fix any problem with locals on the road. This time, though, it would have to be a Tuareg. The nomads ranged across the Sahara and recognized authority beyond their own kind only at the point of a gun. There were not many Tuaregs in Niamey. He would have to ask around.

* * *

The next morning at dawn he was in the back of a flatbed truck headed slowly out of Niamey. The dirt road grew crowded as more trucks rumbled to a start and joined the procession east, like metal beasts rising and moving out from where they had slept. Brown canvas sacks of chickpeas were stacked in the bed of the truck. Wooden posts and slats along the sides kept the sacks from sliding off. A half dozen men sat on top of the sacks as best they could. Issam had a spot near the front where he could rest his back against the cab of the truck.

Issam looked at Moctar, the tall young Tuareg man next to him. He had been in a t-shirt and beige pants when they met last night at a café, common enough clothing in Niamey. Now he wore the traditional Tuareg dress, layered blue robes and a black keffiyeh head wrap. Issam didn't like that he was young, but he came recommended by a Tuareg elder. The old man had assured him, in between quick hissing slurps of sugared tea, that Moctar would do—he came from the right family, had the right connections of kin and influence.

The truck left Niamey on the road to Agadez and the wind buffeted the men in back. Issam slid down against the truck cab, its metal still cool in the early morning sun. The musk of chickpeas mixed with the diesel fumes and dust. He wrapped his cotton keffiyeh across his face.

Plains of brown dirt stretched out from both sides of the asphalt road, their flatness broken by huts of dark mud roofed with branches. Tin panels served as makeshift doors to the huts and flashed the reflected sun as the truck sped by, as if in greeting. A short woman with a bundle of firewood on her head turned away from the truck's dust.

Issam tried not to think about Maram but he felt her letter in his pocket. He shifted against the sacks, but still it pressed against him, like a living, growing thing. An ultimatum, she had dared to give him a deadline. A threat too. Divorce. He knew she was unhappy with him, with all the time he spent in Niger for work. But he hadn't realized she might think to leave him.

The truck slowed to pass a herd of goats on the road. Two young men on the sacks shouted at the shepherd to move his flock. Issam looked over at Moctar. He didn't usually talk to the officials who came with him on these trips. Sometimes the men would talk to him. He remembered the fat one, a clerk in the ministry of civil service he took to Filingué to put a stop to some locals who blocked the road and demanded a tax. Issam drove while the fat clerk talked for five hours straight about movies he had seen.

He had gone to the cinema with Maram during their first year at university in Tripoli. The next year the revolution came and closed the schools, but for that one year they lived free, as modern adults. She was a friend of someone in his math class, but he didn't remember their first meeting. His recollection of Maram began with asking her to the movies and her saying yes. She walked into the theater without hesitation, without talk of chaperones, her eyes meeting his without looking down. He could see that she knew who she was in a way that other women did not, that she knew her own worth. Afterwards they talked politics, like he did with his uncles, except his uncles were not beautiful.

No value, he thought, no value in thinking about the past. He hunched down further against the metal of the truck cab. Go to the tree, negotiate with the Tuareg, and keep the cargo from being seized without anyone getting knifed. Then he could decide about going back to Libya, about trying to make it work with Maram. On balance, he would rather deal with the Tuaregs.

Moctar's hand caught Issam's attention. The Tuareg's long narrow fingers fluttered against one of the sacks, tapping out an intricate rhythm. Moctar looked up at Issam.

"Guitar," he said.

Issam frowned.

Moctar lifted his arms and strummed an invisible instrument.

"Oh," said Issam, "you play guitar?"

"My mother's family is from Mali. They are musicians."

Issam thought to ask how they made money from that, but no, it wouldn't do to offend the young man.

"You play Mali music then?"

Moctar shrugged. "Sometimes. It is not my favorite."

Issam dug his legs down between the sacks. "What is your favorite?" he asked Moctar.

"The American, Jimi Hendrix."

Moctar tapped faster, his fingers a frenzy. He threw his head back, his keffiyeh billowing out from around his face, and howled something incomprehensible into the wind that rushed up from the asphalt and ran over the truck out into the desert. The young Tuareg turned to Issam and smiled, then leaned back against the sacks and closed his eyes.

It was the middle of the day when they stopped for lunch in Agadez. Issam's shirt was damp with sweat. He climbed down stiff-legged from the truck. Boys in shorts ran up and offered to get the men cigarettes and show them to the cafés with the juiciest kebabs and sweetest tea. Behind the boys came old women holding up containers of water and juices, the plastic bottles opaque from age. The women moved their lips rapidly and gestured with the bottles, but they spoke so quietly as to be almost soundless, their sales pitch a whispered incantation.

Issam ignored the boys and avoided making eye contact with the women. He knew the café he wanted and he looked to see if Moctar would join him, but the young Tuareg was already pushing his way through the crowd. Tuaregs probably had their own place to eat here.

A green canvas awning, propped up by poles of metal and wood, shaded the mismatched chairs and tables outside the café. Issam asked the waiter for some paper and made a quick calculation of how much it might cost if they lost the whole load of cargo. It would be a lot, enough to take his salary for the month. He might have to give up more than that even, depending on how much Salah blamed him, depending on whether he reacted as his cousin or as the owner of the business.

The waiter brought his tea and Issam blew on it to cool it off. If he stayed in Niger, he could make the money back soon enough. But Maram had been clear. Even with her letter still in his pocket, he could picture the sentence: "I would never have married you if I had known you would leave me and go to Niger for work." Salah needed him here in Niger and didn't have a job for him in Libya. Maram said her uncle would hire him to run his kiosk in Tripoli. A kiosk. Him, a man of thirty with some university, selling cigarettes. And dealing with her uncle, which meant dealing with her aunt, who never missed a chance to stir up trouble with his family for reasons he had yet to decipher.

Issam sipped his tea and tried to focus on the sensation of stillness. He would be back in the truck soon enough. The tea was brewed from the bark of the moringa tree and tasted a little bitter at first and then very bitter by the end, but it kept away the motion sickness and so he always ordered it in Agadez at the little café with the chairs outside under the green canvas.

There was no pavement after Agadez and the truck followed tire tracks in the compacted sand, picking its way around shallow depressions. The men in back lurched left and right in rhythm with the truck. Out here there were no huts, no people, no trees, just sand tinted sepia by late afternoon sun.

Issam reached into his pocket and took out some dates wrapped in brown paper. He ate one slowly, letting the sweetness linger, and offered them to Moctar. The Tuareg smiled and took one, his fingertips barely touching the sticky brown fruit. Maram made the best magrood cookies with dates, but made him promise not to tell his family that she had baked them. "I don't want them to start thinking of me as your good little housewife. I want to keep them on their toes."

He had expected Maram to be happy when he told her he was going to work with Salah. She had a job at the women's center, doing paperwork for women who couldn't read but needed to file forms with the government, but it didn't pay much. There was good money in the trucking business, enough that they could save to buy a real house and maybe have children. The modern way, like they both wanted. But when he told her about the job, she grabbed his hand and said, "What about us? There is nothing for me in Niger, you know they don't let women there do anything."

They stopped for prayer. The driver's assistant passed around a tall bottle of water and the men washed. A jackal, its brown coat speckled with gray mange, watched from a distance. Issam hoped it would be the short prayer. If he didn't get to the truck tonight the Tuaregs might take matters into their own hands and loot the cargo. Issam stood at one end of the line of men, his arms loose at his sides in the Libyan style, the others crossing their arms in front of them. The driver walked off and pissed in the desert. He was the tallest thing for miles.

*   *   *

It was almost dark when they reached the well where the tree had stood. The driver's assistant leaned out the passenger window and yelled for Issam. Issam and Moctar climbed down from the truck. The truck with its sacks of chickpeas drove off, the dark of the desert swallowing it as Issam watched with the young Tuareg at his side. It was good he had slipped the driver a few more francs, good for the future. It took favors as well as diesel for trucks to make it between Niger and Libya.

"Are you ready?" he asked Moctar.

The young Tuareg wore his headscarf in the traditional manner now, its black folds hiding his face save for his eyes.

"Of course," he said.

There was enough moon to see outlines and shapes, but Issam took out his flashlight, the metal warm in his hand. A group of men approached, moving together as if one. Among them Issam saw Tarek, his bushy hair bouncing as he walked, his round young face catching the dim light of the moon. Next to him was Lotfi, older and skinnier. The rest of the men were Tuareg, their layered robes black in the night though Issam knew them to be indigo, the signature color of these desert nomads.

They exchanged greetings in fragments of French and Arabic. The Tuaregs seemed surprised to see Moctar, and spoke with him. Issam recognized the Tayart language, but couldn't understand what was said.

"I told them we should see the truck first," said Moctar.

Issam nodded and the group walked along the track past a few huts, temporary shelters framed in branches and covered with mats of dry grass. Around them women moved in silence, feeding children and tending camels. In all directions, the empty desert stretched away into darkness.

The men came to where the truck had hit the tree. The cab of the truck twisted down into the earth, the driver's side dug into the sand, the passenger side angled up into the black sky. Under the cab was a dark tangle of wood that seemed part of the vehicle, a growth that tilted the truck off its axis. Issam shone his light along the bed of the truck and saw that the load was still secured, the long metal poles undamaged. Four rocks sat in front of the truck, each about the size of a man's head, a signal that it should not proceed. The Tuaregs must have walked far in these sandy plains to find such rocks, thought Issam. This would be a difficult discussion.

"It is better if I talk with them first," said Moctar.

Issam sat with Tarek and Lotfi on the rocks. Around them the hard dirt of the desert was broken by the upturned roots of the fallen tree. They could hear the Tuaregs talking in the distance where they had gathered around a fire. Issam liked the flowing melodic sound of Tayart, a less guttural cousin of Arabic. He could say a few things in Tayart and the other half-dozen dialects spoken between Niamey and Tripoli. Hello, yes, no, how much? That was enough for his purposes.

The smell of meat cooking over the fire reached them. Issam leaned back on the warm sand and looked up at the black sky salted with stars. It would be nice here if he didn't have to be here. Maybe he would stay in Niger, keep growing the business. Maram would insist on a divorce, but maybe he should cut his losses there, end that tension, even though it would be messy.

Moctar came to them from the Tuaregs' fire. He brought sticks with pieces of meat and handed them to Issam.

"What do they say?" asked Issam.

"We speak about our families and relations."

"And the truck?"

"It is important for us to understand our relationships first."

The young Tuareg's face was covered and Issam could read nothing in his eyes.

"Thank them for the meat."

Moctar left. Issam passed around the sticks and the three men ate. The moon was brighter now. Tarek was trying to read a paperback by the moonlight, a self-help book.

Later, Moctar returned. Tarek put down his book and Lotfi stood.

"Well?" asked Issam.

"The tree was very important to them," said Moctar. "They ask for much compensation."

"Did any of them plant that tree?" Lotfi asked. "No. They did not plant it, their fathers did not plant it. Did any of them water that tree? No. They take their water from here. Does that tree shade their house? No, it shades nothing. They don't care about that tree. It's about money."

Lotfi's eyes darted between the men. Nobody spoke. Lotfi waved his arm and walked off into the night.

The men, Moctar explained, had talked of how they did not use the tree for firewood, did not take its branches to make huts or corrals. It was the only tree for a day's travel in all directions. Nobody knew how the tree had come to grow here, so far from any others. Clearly it was here for a purpose, though even the elders could not say what that purpose might be. The Tuaregs left the tree alone, and it had come to mark the track to Agadez.

"I think I should speak to them now," said Issam.

Moctar nodded and they went over and sat with the Tuaregs around the fire.

Issam looked around at each of the men, their faces covered, eyes reflecting back the dancing firelight. He counted four styles of scarf folds, so four different family lineages represented around the fire. That would make for complicated negotiations. Three of the men seemed older, their robes looser, their feet wrinkled with deeper creases. The old men will be the ones to decide, thought Issam. That is always how it is everywhere.

Issam took a deep breath and, with Moctar translating, explained his business, how he worked for his cousin, how accidents were going to happen, but that for the flow of goods to continue— for the cheap sandals the men wore, for the soap their women used—the trucks had to continue. In four years they had grown from one truck to three, and yes, there had been accidents, like the tree, but they had always stopped and come to an agreement with the local people, kept their blessing to pass through their land without trouble. Now they needed to come to a reasonable arrangement here so his business could continue. He presented his proposal, that he would give them a small sum in compensation and a metal pole to erect in place of the tree, so there would still be a landmark to navigate by.

His short speech catalyzed a flurry of Tayart, the men talking over each other, Moctar weighing in, gesturing, his metal bracelets catching the light from the fire.

Issam scooped up a handful of sand and let it run through his fingers. The Tuaregs kept arguing.

One of the old men threw his arms up in the air, flicking his wrists and looking away as he did so. Issam recognized the gesture. His father, ever stubborn, used it to dismiss even the most logical argument. Then his uncle would start bellowing, much like the short Tuareg across from him was doing now. He had hated dealing with all that, detested it even when his family had deployed their mix of stubbornness and bluster to help get him and Salah the permits for the trucks. And now more of that waited for him in Tripoli, if he went back. Issam grabbed another handful of sand and squeezed it hard before throwing it behind him. It had been a long day.

"Moctar," he said. "What is the problem here?"

Moctar turned and whispered to Issam in Arabic. "There are some problems between the different families in this group. Your proposal is reasonable. The trouble is with how they divide things between themselves."

That was the problem with the old ways, Issam thought, here or in Tripoli. In the narrow world defined by kin you couldn't get anything done without tripping over a dusty family argument. He was tired and enough was enough.

"Look, this is business," said Issam, standing up. He addressed the circle of Tuaregs in Arabic he knew they wouldn't understand: "Your family issues do not concern me."

Issam felt two distinct beats of his heart. On the third beat, the short Tuareg went from sitting empty-handed to standing in front of him with a knife. The long curving arc of the blade glowed red in the firelight and Issam stepped back. The Tuareg leapt forward, cursing him in Arabic, and Issam sucked in his breath as the knife vanished. He saw only deep dark blue, then felt soft fabric pressed against his face and heard Moctar speaking fast Tayart. He tensed, waiting for the pain to come, but no, Moctar had stepped in front of him, grabbed the arm holding the knife. Issam backed away from the circle of Tuareg men. They were standing now and talking in low insistent voices, their hands holding and calming his would-be killer. Nobody was paying any attention to him.

Issam walked back toward the truck. His hands shook. To steady them he picked up a stick from the ground and gripped it hard. He didn't think they would kill him now. That had been the moment, but Moctar had come through for him, he was loyal. The stick snapped in his hands and startled him. He sat down heavy on one of the rocks. Tarek and Lotfi were gone. He supposed they had found somewhere to sleep.

He had pictured himself dying, but never here, not out in the desert, not alone like this. Would anyone have thought to look for him? His cousin, he supposed. There was the truck after all. Tarek might care. Not Lotfi. And Maram, who knew with her. He hadn't been home in five months. Her letter said she hadn't given up on him, but he didn't know if he believed her. He remembered the way she spoke about some of the bad husbands of the women she helped at the center. Maybe she spoke that way about him now, maybe she would prefer he not return from the desert. The possibility hurt his stomach and brought sweat to his palms. He didn't know what to do about her.

The night air had grown cold and the women and children were asleep in the huts when Moctar returned to where Issam sat by the truck.

"It is settled," he told Issam. "If you will also pay the men for their labor, they will accept your proposal. Because I am asking them to, and as we have the right relationships."

Issam sighed and stood, his legs unsure. "Yes, fine. Thank you for taking my side, not letting him kill me."

"I am not on your side. I am Tuareg. But if you die, I don't get paid."

Issam stared at him. He was serious. "Good business decision then." Issam rubbed his head. "Tell them I accept."

He would take one of the metal poles from the truck cargo and leave it here. Even with that loss, the shipment of poles would still be profitable enough. With the next truck he would send concrete to make a base for the pole, and shovels to dig a hole where the tree had stood. The Tuareg would leave four men here to do the labor and he would pay them. A metal pole five meters high would replace the tree, a permanent landmark in place of a fragile one.

Issam made a quick estimate of the total cost in francs and converted it to Libyan jneh. It was not an expensive agreement as these things went. Tuaregs rarely had a chance to earn cash, so they would be happy with the modest sum. Moctar would probably ask for a bigger fee when they got back to Niamey, but he would hold him to the original price.

Issam found Tarek behind the truck, reading again by flashlight.

"It is settled," Issam told him.

"Good."

"How did you and Lotfi hit the tree?"

"Lotfi is not himself. He had some problem at home, with his family, before we left. He was telling me about it and not looking."

Jackals yowled in the distance, their high-pitched cries rising in unison.

"I will drive us to Niamey," Tarek continued. "Then I think he will be okay."

Issam shook his head. You never knew if someone would be okay if the problem was at home. He remembered when it started to go bad with Maram. It was maybe one year into the trucking business and he had just walked in to their flat in Tripoli after two months in Niamey. She was peeling potatoes and he watched as the brown slivers slid into the sink in a rhythm that stayed steady in the silence.

"Okay," said Issam. "Tell Lotfi we will talk about this when we are back in Niamey."

He claimed the truck cab as his sleeping quarters for the night. The seat wasn't tilted too badly and he could lock the doors. He felt the truck settle as he got in, its weight pressing down on the tree, the broken wood creaking. The plastic of the seat was cool against his body. He closed his eyes and pictured how the tree had looked years ago, the first time he was here. The acacia rose out of the desert and stood solitary against an endless plain of sand and rock. The main trunk slanted upward at an angle then split into two branches that swerved back in the other direction, a bundle of green leaves on top. It looked to him like a dancer leaning forward and throwing her arms up in the air behind her, holding a child up to the sky.

Issam half-woke as dawn light entered the tilted cab. He thought of Maram and leaned his face against the top of her head. Her hair smelled like walnuts, and she smiled at him as he rubbed her arms under her favorite blue djellaba. He would ask her to make the magrood cookies when he got back to Tripoli. That would be a good place to start. His eyes stung and he closed them. He floated up into the sky and looked down at the tree below him. The wind took him higher and he watched the tree get ever smaller until it was a single green dot in a vast brown desert.

DAVID DEGUSTA is an MFA student in fiction at the Iowa Writers' Workshop where he is working on a novel. His writing has appeared in Boulevard, Catapult, *and* The Normal School, *among other places. He also translates from Amharic, the national language of Ethiopia. He can be found online at www.davidwrites.net or on Twitter @davidwrites1.*

Barely a Sound

Kathleen Latham

There was barely a sound when the baby fell into the pool. No squeak of surprise on the baby's part. No cry of alarm from the grown-ups. Nothing to mark the enormity of the event. Just the faintest of splashes.

Libby was sitting by the pool with Curtis and her dad when it happened.

It was day three of their first vacation since Mom had left, and they were all doing their best to pretend things were normal. Her dad was on his laptop as usual, his face scrunched in that embarrassing squint he made when he stared at the screen, chunky headphones on top of his head—the kind you're supposed to wear to block out noise but he seemed to need everywhere now, even on vacation in Puerto Rico, apparently.

Her brother was stretched out on the lounge chair beside him, long legs crossed, earbuds in, eyes closed. Only the year before, he would have spent the entire day playing games with Libby. Stupid, Curtis-games, like the one where they took turns saying *penis* louder and louder until their parents told them to stop. Now all he wanted to do was listen to crappy rap music and look for WiFi so he could text his girlfriend, the one with big boobs and a mean face who treated Libby like she was mentally deficient. Which meant Libby had nothing to do but sit there, watching people. Something she did a lot of lately.

Ms. Friel, the middle school counselor, said Libby was having trouble *settling in* since her mom had left. As if your mom running off with the guy who fixes your cars is something you can settle into. Like a chair. Or a new house.

"This is your new normal," Ms. Friel liked to say. "The sooner you accept it, the better."

Which was missing the point, Libby thought. Six months ago, if anyone had asked, she would have said her parents were as happily married as anyone else. There were no obvious signs of trouble. No blow-up fights. No throwing of dishes or crying behind closed doors. Nothing that spoke of saying good-bye. But it wasn't like her mom just woke up one day and decided, *Hey, I think I'll trade in my husband and two kids for the guy who gave me a discount on my wiper blades.* Which meant Libby had missed something. Some vital clue that could have told her what was about to happen. And if that was true, what other disasters might be waiting to ambush her?

So, she watched people. All the time. Her body simmered with the tension of it. Like she was one of those air traffic control people in charge of preventing another crash.

"Stop being weird," Curtis had said on their first day at the hotel. "You can't just sit and stare at people."

But she couldn't help herself. The more she watched, the more she noticed details she had never noticed before. Like how some people barely looked at the person they were with, and others couldn't keep their hands off them—a steadying hand on the back as they climbed onto a stool at the swim-up bar; a pinky finger touching a thigh as they both pretended to sleep.

She liked to group the guests into categories: young/old, happy/ sad, married/dating, mother/father. When she got tired of that, she broke those groups down into subsets: skinny dads, overweight dads, dads who threw their kids into the pool, dads like her own, who still seemed to be at work. The moms at the pool were harder to sort. They all seemed the same to Libby—soft women with pouchy bellies and dimpled thighs who spent their entire day reading and never set foot in the water.

After a while, she felt like the narrator in one of those nature shows her dad made her watch: *Here we have that colorful species, man with facial hair and tattoos, lying beside his female counterpart, girl with belly piercing and baseball cap. Nearby, at the bar, sits woman with sunburn. Note how she gets louder and louder the longer she's there.*

On the second day, a blonde family had appeared like gazelles creeping shyly from the shadows. Two young boys and their parents, all of them straight-backed and tall and ridiculously beautiful. Dutch, Libby thought. Or Danish. Or maybe those were the same; she wasn't sure. They only stayed a short time, sitting perfectly still on the edge of their seats as if fulfilling some duty, before filing out again to go play tennis or ride a yacht or whatever it was people like that did. Libby thought they looked sad, but maybe that was a Dutch thing too.

The only girls near Libby's age had been two dark-skinned girls with dazzling smiles and beaded braids who spent their entire time in the water, splashing and laughing, calling to each other in a language Libby didn't understand. She had wanted to swim with them, but she couldn't be sure they weren't laughing at her, so she stayed in the deep end instead, treading water, clinging to the edge when she got tired. They hadn't been back since.

The point was, she was paying attention. All the time. Which was why she noticed the baby and her family as soon as they entered the pool area.

There was no dad, just a mom carrying the baby and a grandmother holding the hand of a boy of about three who scuffed his green Crocs across the deck as though he didn't want to be there. They were Indian, Libby thought, because the grandmother wore one of those pretty robe things that draped across her shoulder. Or maybe that was racist. Maybe people in other countries wore those too. Again, Libby wasn't sure.

The mom led the way to a cluster of empty lounge chairs where she set the baby down with an audible groan, as if she had carried her a great distance. The baby stood on her own, bow-legged and bouncy, one hand on a lounge chair for balance. She looked old enough to walk, but barely. Which made her what? Libby wondered. One? One-and-a-half? Libby was pretty sure she was a girl because she wore a pink one-piece with black dolphins dancing across it and tiny gold studs in her ears. Libby's own parents had made her wait until her twelfth birthday to get her ears pierced, which was ridiculously old, so she noticed the earrings with a mixture of envy and wonder.

While the baby bopped up and down, the mom unpacked a beach bag stuffed with enough towels, floaties, and toys to entertain a preschool, and the grandmother set about slathering suntan lotion onto the boy who squirmed so much she had to hold him by the wrist. They had their backs to the baby, Libby noticed. Not in a mean way, just like they were busy.

The baby didn't seem to care. She had caught sight of the pool and stood staring at it, transfixed. Libby imagined what that expanse of gleaming water looked like to her. A vast ocean of light, maybe. A shimmering blue carpet. The baby lifted her pudgy little arms and wiggled her fingers as if calling for it. Then she took a step forward.

By now, the mom had joined in the corralling of the little boy, scolding him with clucking sounds and holding his shoulders while the grandmother rubbed lotion onto his back. Libby felt a flash of superiority at that, because really, why should it take two people to put suntan lotion on a person and god help him when he got to middle school and had to do things for himself like learn algebra and deal with lockers and bullies and stuff.

The baby took another step. Then another.

She's toddling, Libby thought, the word jumping into her head. That's what the awkward little steps looked like. Toddles.

Toddle. Toddling. Toddler.

Libby was thinking about those words the way you do when you realize something you've said your whole life isn't just random but is linked to something else when the baby walked into the water.

Step. Step. In.

Just like that.

As if the wavy blue surface before her was nothing more than a continuation of the ground that up until then had kept her safe. She sank instantly.

Libby didn't know why she thought babies would flounder if they fell in the water. That they'd wave their arms and splutter and cough. She was so certain of it that when the baby dropped out of sight—as quickly and surely as if the water had swallowed her whole—it took her a moment to process what had happened. She sat up a little, to check, and sure enough, there was the baby on the bottom of the pool. Arms floating at her sides. Legs moving slightly as though she were walking down the bottom's steady slope.

Libby hesitated. Only for a second, but it was a long second.

Long enough to consider the possibility that this was one of those wonder babies who could actually swim, and she might burst from the water at any moment and start paddling. Long enough to give the mom a chance to turn around. For the grandmother to notice. Long enough for any other adult to spot the little pink bathing suit dotted with dolphins walking on the bottom of the pool. But the mom and the grandmother were battling the brother. And over at the bar, the grown-ups had their backs turned, and the bartender was pouring from a bottle held at shoulder height, and the waitress was tapping on a register, and around the pool, the sunbathers had their eyes closed, or were looking at their phones, or their books, or their tablets, and no one noticed. No one was paying attention. Only Libby.

Maybe she yelled. Or called for help. She wasn't sure. The next thing she knew, she was in the water.

It was cold, shockingly cold. It churned around her, blurring her vision, and for a moment she worried about losing the contacts she'd just been deemed old enough to wear. But then she spotted the pink suit and a fuzzy cap of black hair and she kicked forward until her fingertips brushed against bathing suit. She hooked the baby with one arm—her little body surprisingly solid and compact—then, adrenaline pounding, pushed off the bottom of the pool with more force than necessary, exploding into sunlight and shouting. By now the mother and grandmother had noticed, and Libby was barely to the edge before they ripped the baby out of her arms, crying and jabbering in yet another language Libby didn't understand.

"She fell in," she told them, wiping water from her face.

But the women were too busy fussing over the baby who wasn't making any sound at all. Horror seized Libby by the throat. Shouldn't she be crying? Or choking? Or coughing? For one terrifying second, she thought she'd been too late, that the baby had drowned, and a horrible chasm of guilt opened up before her, an expanse so deep, she knew that if she fell into it, she'd never climb back out.

But then the grandmother turned and said something to Libby over and over and the mother stopped kissing the baby's face long enough for Libby to see the baby staring down at her calmly, blinking water from her eyes, looking a little confused by all the fuss.

Libby took a breath, her heart banging in her chest. "She fell in," she tried again.

No one else at the pool seemed aware of what had happened. A few people looked up at the commotion with annoyed frowns, but Libby's voice was swallowed up by the whirring of blenders and the babbling at the bar and the cheesy island music being piped through speakers that looked like rocks. She stood in the water awkwardly, worried that she would somehow be blamed.

Finally, the baby had enough and started to cry and the grandmother wrapped her in a towel and there was a lot of bowing at Libby from the mom and staring by the little boy and the scooping up of toys and more of the language she didn't understand, and then the two women grabbed the brother by the hand and whisked both kids away, leaving Libby standing in the pool, strangely disappointed. As if saving the baby wasn't enough and what she really wanted was for the mother and grandmother to say, "You are an amazing girl. You have done an amazing thing." But of course, no one talks like that. Or maybe they do. Maybe that's what they were saying, and Libby just didn't know it.

She hoisted herself out of the water and went back to her seat. Her dad and Curtis hadn't changed positions. She stood over them, hunched and dripping. "Did you see that?" she asked, her voice shaking.

Neither of them looked at her.

"Dad," she said, kicking his lounge chair with her foot.

He looked up in surprise, half a squint still visible on his face.

"Did you see me save the baby?"

He didn't bother to take off his headphones. "What?"

"Did you see me save the baby?"

"Baby?"

Libby looked across the empty pool, its surface calm now, the people around it back to looking elsewhere. "There was a baby," she said, less confidently.

Her dad's eyes slid downward, as if checking to make sure his laptop hadn't disappeared. "Uh-huh."

"Can you move?" Curtis said. "You're getting me wet."

Libby opened her mouth to argue, then stopped. She desperately wanted to tell them what had happened, but without the baby there as proof, she was pretty sure her brother would turn it into something to tease her about. Like, *Remember when Libby tried to tell us she saved a baby?* And her father would smile sadly and tell him to stop, and he'd say he believed her in a way that distinctly meant he didn't, and her mom…well, clearly, Libby had no idea what her mom would do.

Suddenly, she felt cold, despite the sun beating down on her. She retreated back to the water and slipped in quietly, huddling against the side, embarrassed, though she wasn't sure why. From across the pool, a bald man in a lounge chair toasted her with his pina colada, which felt creepy, so she turned her back on him and pretended to study the blue and white squares of the pool tiles. Self-doubt prickled the back of her neck.

How long would it take a baby to drown anyway? Two minutes? Three? Plenty of time for the mother and grandmother to notice. Plenty of time for them to scoop her up themselves.

Maybe this kind of thing happened all the time—babies wandering away from their mothers, mothers pulling them back. Maybe the women hadn't been thanking her at all. Maybe they were telling her to mind her own business and keep her hands off their baby.

Libby let go of the edge and let herself sink. Made herself heavy and helpless.

She meant to count. To see how long she could last, how long the baby might have lasted. But somewhere between twelve and thirteen, loneliness swept over her and a memory came of a time when she and her mom had sat watching a family of ducks skim across the surface of a sunlit pond, the downy ducklings trailing their mother as if on a string.

"Can baby ducks drown?" Libby had asked.

Her mother had smiled. "No, they're born knowing what to do."

Later, Libby found out this wasn't exactly true. Baby ducks could drown for a number of reasons.

She thought of this now. She thought of the invisible string tethering those ducks to their mother. And the baby in the dolphin-spotted suit being covered in kisses. She thought about the lies adults tell, even when they don't mean to.

And mostly what she felt was alone.

Alone on the bottom of the pool, with the water all around her and the distorted view of the sky above and a muffled silence that was not quite silence filling her ears and a nagging, unavoidable need to breathe building in her chest.

Why did everything have to be so hard?

Anger came then. Rage at the burning contradiction of everything she felt. Wanting to be noticed, but not singled out. Loved, but left alone. Wanting her life to go back to how it was, but also wanting to hurtle forward, skipping all the years she knew were coming.

She wanted, she wanted, she wanted.

And meanwhile, her mind kept going back to what had just happened and the words she couldn't understand and the details that kept accumulating like a map without a key, until it was too much to be sunk on the bottom—like a rock, like a shell, like a dead thing—and before she could make a conscious choice, her legs flexed and an underwater scream propelled her upwards, air bubbles popping with fury, and she broke through the surface, greedy lungs delivering her to sunlight.

She gasped at the shock of breathing.

At the righteous misery of wanting more.

KATHLEEN LATHAM has won the Web Microfiction Prize for Women Writers and the Writer's Digest *Short Short Story Competition and has been a finalist for* Shenandoah's *Bevel Summers Prize for Short Fiction and* Southeast Review's *World's Best Short Short Story Competition. Her fiction has appeared in such places as* 100 Word Story, Crack the Spine Literary Magazine, Flash Fiction Magazine, *and* Fictive Dream. *Her poetry has appeared in numerous anthologies and journals such as* Tipton Poetry Journal *and* Constellations. *Born and raised in Southern California, she now lives outside of Boston, Massachusetts with her husband and an ornery cat. You can find her on social media at @lathamwithapen or online at KathleenLatham.com*

Egging

Sophia Zaklikowski

E ven through the daylong night the murres continued their
cawing. Lydia lay awake, a rattling wind weaving through
the colony's vicious chorus. In her first weeks on the island, she
soothed herself that she would adjust—the bird calls would
sound as ordinary as a clock ticking out every second of every
day in the corner of a room—but nine months in, she still was
not accustomed to their awful, constant crying, something like a
smoker's sore laugh.

Before marrying Amos, until she was twenty, Lydia had lived with
her parents in San Francisco—a boisterous outpost of loud drunk
men and arguing men and yelling vendors and clomping horses,
and there she found with time her ear whittled down the noise into
something smooth. But here, on these islands, the Farallones, she
heard the birds and their untranslatable lament always.

She rose out of bed. The room was tar black, no windows. No
windows, yet still wet inside. No escaping the interminable damp
of the island—sea spray spit up from below, fog sweat down from
above. Lydia hiked wool stockings up her legs, lazily holding them

up at her thighs, not yet bothered to tie them into place, slipped into wooden clogs and then outside.

Through an empty pocket in the fog a thread of ember orange stitched the horizon onto the deep indigo of everywhere else. Below, where the eggers camped in waxed tents, a few lanterns pinpricked the night: early-rising men or men who also couldn't sleep amidst the terrific roaring of the murres. Dawn, or close enough to it to not return to sleep.

Lydia stared at the horizon, the glowing prelude to the rising sun. She stared right into it. Deep strange neon. It was the bloody color of the murre's yolk, and making this association, a tired dread rose in a flush through her body. Another samely day. Soon, she'd be cracking those eggs into a pan for breakfast, two for her husband, one for her, the whites never quite whitening, retaining their glossy embryonic sheen. And later for lunch, and later for supper. It was a luxury, she knew—for the general lack of chickens in California, miners and town-folk and the Russians up at Fort Ross paid good money for these eggs, up to a dollar per in slim times out of season—but despite the shame in knowing that, she was sick of them, sick of their richness and fishy flavor, and sicker at how everything was the same, her life on this island one of constants and continuals: the landscape without so much as a tree, the stench of split eggs and guano, sea lion and man stink, the steep hillsides and the ache in her knees, the brittle rocks which scored her stockings and tagged her ankles in raised scrapes, the gray wet sky and the gray wet ocean, the seabirds and nothing but seabirds, the men and nothing but men.

When she'd first arrived after the harrowing boat trip from the San Francisco bay, the rotten heat of her own bile in her mouth, she was introduced to another woman, Mrs. Brambilla. Her husband was a leadman, like Amos. Together they oversaw the eggers, managed their dissent and nostalgia and disagreements, counted each day's collected bounty, and carefully packed them into crates for their turbulent journey to port.

Mrs. Brambilla had lived on the Farallones with her husband for four years–her skin was jerkied like the men's, and Lydia saw in her split-vein cheeks and seasick eyes a vision of the future. But Mrs. Brambilla wasn't nearly as haggard as her suffered face suggested. She was sturdy and loud—Catholic. Lydia worked in Mrs. Brambilla's shadow, following her around the feral island, and as they went to and fro, Mrs. Brambilla would joke with the eggers, telling raunchy jokes in her vestigial Italian accent, the prudish and the young still pimply boys blushing at her cussing. Lydia would carry heavy buckets of ocean water for washing up the hillsides, Mrs. Brambilla spanking her bottom like it was the haunch of a mule from behind. The woman drank cup after cup of sour coffee, a pot of water always at a boil. She taught Lydia where the water's edge was too dangerous to near, and showed her how the pointed murre eggs spun like a child's top rather than rolled, so that if they fell out of the nest they wouldn't tumble down the cliffs. Of the avian stench and symphony she promised, *You get used to it.* Once, they spent an odd sunny afternoon laying in a cove together, their backs pressed into the round stones, and Mrs. Brambilla hiked up her blouse to sun her stomach, paying no notice to Lydia, who looked on at her doughy middle rise and fall with breath—flesh the palest olive tone, color of stone lichen—and then noted the woman's face: the barely-there smile of someone with a secret, how her eyelids didn't flutter, even at the touch of beach flies coming and going from her skin. And Lydia did the same, opened the clasps of her cloistering top and rolled up the camisole beneath it, and the two women lay flat on the beach, beacon bellies shining. After a month, Mrs. Brambilla fell ill and fevered to death and with her Lydia's sole kinship died too—she was now the only woman. Lydia wept herself to sleep, face down into her mattress to stifle her cries from Amos across the room in his bed, thankful for once for the birds, for their incessant wailing which buried hers.

Lydia wasn't as outgoing or brash as Mrs. Brambilla, nor was she as matronly. The egger men sucked their lips and said foul things at her as she passed. No one as of yet had touched her—for fear of her husband, their boss, surely—but once as she was walking she spied a man across the way on a bluff watching her, his hand working his penis, a vibrating spot of flesh at his center, his face indistinct at the distance. She looked away immediately and quickened her pace, but still she felt his gaze on her the whole way back up the little mountain and furthermore knew that her very discomfort was what excited him. In this way she participated in his pleasure.

More camp lights turned on below. A cold wind flipped up off the ridge and into Lydia's bare face. She winced. The uppermost cap of the sun was now visible bobbing like a buoy at the edge of the Pacific. Lydia turned to start water for the day. Was sick too of sunrise.

*   *   *

Amos came out an hour later, rounded his way into the outdoor kitchen, sheltered atop by a large slab of redwood bark imported from the mainland.

Lydia had a cup of coffee ready for him, with sugar, which she allowed a ration of for herself on Saturdays which was not today.

"Provisions come in today," he said.

She said she knew.

"Don't go through the cornmeal so fast this time."

She nodded, stirring a cornmeal batter smooth.

Lydia's father, a baker, had switched to buying murre eggs when chickens became hard to come by. In this way the two men became acquainted. One morning in the off season during a stay in the city, Amos—a year widowed—saw Lydia working behind the counter. Glass cases containing buns and pastries refracted light throughout the room and the pale gemming light caught on her eyes—wet with youth, burnt brown freckled with red, like a shimmery piece of dulse. She didn't smile with her teeth except on accident in which case he might've spied little yellow beads arranged flat and straight. He asked her on a stroll; they walked around her neighborhood and he bought her an orange and watched as she ate it, turned half away from him, slice by slice. Its fragrance filled the space between them. On his following visit to the city, soon after, he asked for her hand.

"I was thinking," Amos said between sips of hot coffee, "how about you come down with me to look at the pelts they bring to peddle with them's provisions? I may have even asked them specially to bring some women's coats last time around." He pinched her waist. "You're getting skinny cause you're too cold, shiverin' all the time."

"What time?" she asked.

"I'll come up't get you."

"Roundabouts when?" She covered the batter in a rag and pushed it aside.

"You know those boats are never on schedule. Only the devil's on schedule."

"So I just sit around then?"

"That's right," he said. "You just sit pretty for once." He smiled a big smile, revealing his sickly blossom-pink gums. She said nothing more.

Amos ate and left. Lydia drank the sweetened cold dregs of his sour coffee and rinsed the cup and the rest of their dishes in saltwater, set them to dry on the stone slab next to the washbowl. Crystals of salt crusted everything, the plates and forks and knives, and inside their home it webbed across her hand mirror and hairbrush, and in her hair it clung to each strand like gloves of crisp lace.

As a girl, Lydia had sucked her thumb, craving the lick of salt so ready at her hand. Her mother took to dipping them in ink pots to cull the habit. Now, Lydia tasted salt always; the air was swollen with it.

Despite Lydia's dismay, she was indeed happy to have left her parents. Her sad, distant father and her taciturn, bitter mother. That was perhaps her problem, that no matter where she was, Lydia would be dissatisfied. She wrote in her diary that she had grass is always greener syndrome. For what did she want? If she could have anything, what would it be? She used to want to sing opera, as a childhood fancy. Other girls her age wanted to become teachers, or mothers. She likely would become a mother, but it wasn't something she wanted. So why not a godforsaken island, with cliffs like razors, infested with miserable, desperate cawing birds and their shit everywhere, dried and fresh, and mice stowed over on boats, marooned, mating so profusely that the earth literally crawled with them, their burrowing bodies visible beneath the clumped ground, surrounded by white sharks which bloodied the waters offshore inciting violent feeding frenzies of gulls above the crimson-stained ocean, bits of sealion later washing up on the rocky wrack line with the usual jellyfish goo and slimy whips of kelp? Why not wish for, of all the things in the world, an otter pelt coat and a sugarcube on Saturdays? Why not dream of a husband still mourning his late-wife to make quick huffy love to by candlelight come evening, the room smelling of sperm, floral and fecund, and spermaceti, like whey, softly fecal? And besides, sometimes she did feel content. Sometimes she saw the shallows turn turquoise under rare sunlight or noticed a whale's breath fountain further out where the ocean appeared flat, solid, and dark as a fry pan. Sometimes after Amos finished grunting in the nape of her neck, they'd lie together and he would hum a whimsical song and use two fingers to perform a jig on the curve of her hip and she would laugh at the simulacrum legs shimmying across her skin. Sometimes she loved her parents, felt their faces on her face, felt their heartaches in her heart, felt she loved them more now with some fathom between them. Sometimes her breast ached for a babe who she envisioned growing up calloused and salted, who would love and understand this godforsaken island for it had raised them. So yes, why not?

She finished washing up. It was far too early in the day for the boat to arrive, which probably left port in San Francisco at dawn, at the same time she woke up to the yoke of the sun breaking into the bowl of the sky. With no sense in waiting around all morning, Lydia donned herself in wool, exchanged her wooden shoes for leather lace-up ones, and left to walk around.

It was early March; the island was green. An herbaceous seaplant with low-lying alien daisies bloomed everywhere, dotting the flatter areas of the island yellow. Downy feathers stuck in the petals quivered like tinsel at her ankles. Higher up on the crags, nothing could grow. The scribbled skyline was brown and barren, painted in great swaths of white guano. Lydia set straight out from her house towards the highest peak she could see.

Only a handful of walkways weaved across the entire island, singletrack footpaths worn into dust which led from dock to house, house to lookout, house to water, water to dock, dock to campground, campground to egg fields. Once at the egg fields, there were no real paths. All the eggs were high along the steepest cliffs, tucked into granite shelves, requiring scrappy footwork from the eggers. The black-winged white-bodied murres roosted there, laddering up from curdling ocean to gauzed sky, watching from obsidian-bead eyes their eggs get plucked from the forever-until-now protective wall.

The sky split. Flimsy sunlight leaked through, hitting in beams just where Lydia walked. It continued in a silver line up the hill and she decided to follow it. The murre hollered and behind their gurgled cacaws gulls screamed pitchy. Lydia paused and really listened. Closed her eyes and tried to pick out one distinct voice among the million. Then she opened her mouth and pumped her lungs in a way she hadn't since she used to sing, mimicking the strange sorrowful cackle—*muhhhr hur hur hur hur hur! Muhhr hur hur hur hur hur!* She laughed at herself and kept on.

*   *   *

After a half hour or so of walking, the incline growing, the sun fogged over again and her sundust road disappeared. Never mind, she was near the top of a pitched rock steeple.

Along the scarp she used her hands to guide her, skirting around boulders like a four-legged beast. The wind picked up, humming in her ear, the whole world a seashell held up to her temple.

At the top of the spiked peak, she could see out in every direction. It was as if she sat at the top of a hat, could see the brim of the island upon which men scuttled. Beyond that another brim, the horizon—circular perimeter where ocean froth and fog fall into each other, the day too gray to see the mainland to the east. Amidst the uniformity of the drizzly landscape, a colorful patch caught Lydia's eye on a plateau a few dozen feet below her.

She wound her way down to it, feeling agile now among the rocks.

Like a little stage, the plateau was perfectly flat, a rectangle about the size of her and Amos's house. On the three sides other than the side from which she'd descended, the land dropped off. Feeling wily, she tiptoed to an edge and peered down. Birds circled in layers.

She couldn't recall ever being up so high, looking down so far. A breeze flooded up from the cliff's underbelly and she almost felt sick. Retreating, Lydia went to examine the colorful pile that had attracted her down in the first place, nervous to turn her back on the plummeting expanse, as if a giant murre might shoot up from hiding beneath the lip of the rock, peck at the hem of her skirt, and tug her down into a feathery grave.

The pile was mostly flowers. The heads of those strange yellow daisies, petals wilted, sucked dry by the salt air. Also some purple and red ones, rarer on the island. Shards of opalescent abalone. Sea-smooth stones, colored auburn, maroon, jade, and slate. And a knobbed and fingered staff of driftwood driven into the earth with another smaller piece twined perpendicular to it—a cross.

Lydia did not yet know much about her husband Amos, let alone about Amos's first wife. She knew that Mary had lived on the island for several years. Mrs. Brambilla had known her. They were good friends. Mrs. Brambilla mentioned her in passing from time to time: *This is Mary's recipe; Mary could row a boat to Seal Rock faster than any of them boys; Mary did Mr. Amos's clothes like so.* Lydia knew these things about Mary. She also knew that she was dead and that Amos missed her. She knew this from the first time she met Amos, twice her age and stinky, from the heartsick guilt obvious on his face as her father introduced them. He probably still loved her and would likely never love Lydia that way, though he'd be decent and devoted to her. Lydia knew this and she also knew that the manner of Mary's death was violent—that she had fallen to her death.

This had been relayed to her on the boat ride from San Francisco to the Farallones. Before she was a mess of vomit, she sat beside a man with white hair and caking skin returning for the egging high season. He spoke nonstop of his gold mining endeavors, how close he'd come to riches, he knew the vein was good, but he blew his savings and would have to return next year, after this egging season. He warned her of the stench she'd live through in the first week, for at the start of each season the laborers dutifully bludgeoned all of the eggs they found to ensure only fresh ones were then available for harvest, cloaking the whole island in putrid sulfuric rot. He told her many ghost stories and scant love stories and an encyclopedia of egger gossip that bored her terribly. But she perked back up when he started in on Mary, lovely Mary who fell to her death. The churn of the ocean had started to infect Lydia with churn—she pushed the rising tide in her stomach down in the hopes of hearing a bit more of her predecessor, but even this chatty old egger didn't say much, just fingered his stringy beard and shook his head.

Men died in this way each year, falling from the precarious perches along the cliff sides, their backs shattering as easily as eggshells. Danger—death—was simply the nature of the job. Like mining or lumbering or birthing. But Mary wasn't an egger. Lydia had not heard it spelled out as such, nor would she ever be so bold as to ask, but she believed that Mary's death was not accidental, that she had decidedly plunged.

Lydia looked at the heap of treasures and wished beyond wishing that she could speak with Mary, share in the experience of isolation living on this forgotten chunk of land, the musty odor of cracked eggs on the rocks, the sad cries of their mothers, the samely days full of work with nowhere to go and no one to see but men, men seeing them, and Amos, Amos always asking, and Amos a man too. She wished beyond wishing to have a friend and be a friend. To sit talking with guano-stained bottoms on cold hard rocks and be on this island together.

She would need to be this for herself. She would split herself in two, maybe three. With several of herself, she hoped, she wouldn't get sick of herself, too.

*   *   *

It was surely nearing noon. Lydia took the downhill in big falling strides. Approaching her home, she became anxious that Amos would be waiting for her, that she would have to explain her outing. She jogged lightly for the last portion, but to her relief he wasn't there. The fog had burned off slightly and more of the ocean was visible. A wide aluminum plate. One boat yond like a piece of pepper on the plate. She set to boiling eggs.

Amos returned home not long after to Lydia cross-stitching idly. They ate the boiled eggs with red beans and each drank a cup of dark ale. She combed his hair back for him, checking for lice as she went, put on a finer dress, and they left to meet the shipment.

*   *   *

Provision hauls came in every other month. They advertised butter, meal, linen, thread, bacon, tea, macaroni, beans, sugar, shoes, soap, coffee, books, magazines, bibles, nails, matches, tobacco, baskets, yeast, knives, axes, condensed milk, dried peaches, ropes, utensils, dehydrated vegetables, (wilting) fresh vegetables, potatoes, blankets, bullets, underwear, wax, canvas, candles, paper, charcoal, ink, whiskey, wine, ale, and pelts. Some things or others were always unavailable. Everything was expensive.

All of the few dozen men living on the island flocked the dock. Amos led his wife by the arm through the uproar, the raucous shouting eggers and the yapping seabirds above, flying in halos above the boat, waiting for an attack.

Amos spoke to the vendor and asked for the pelts, specifically the coats which he'd requested. The man returned in several trips with piles of otter and fur seal pelts, most well longer than Lydia was tall. Lydia saw seals often and eggers killed them for their fur, but they didn't skin and tan them as beautifully as the Russians up north at Fort Ross. The otter pelts were a whole other story. She'd never felt anything so soft. It made sense why they'd all been killed off round the islands—softer than scalp, than silk, than her own cheek down which she rubbed on the backside of her knuckles to lull herself to sleep.

Her husband started speaking with the vendor in a lower register, implying sternness, a trade to come. As they spoke, he held coat after coat, cape after cape, up to Lydia's frame. She held out her arms so that he could measure the sleeves. The fur shone almost purple in the light.

Lydia thought of the women at Fort Ross. She wondered how the odor of otter meat and seal blubber traveled from the slaughter beaches into the palisades. At all hours of the day, sea lion barks sounded throughout the Farallones, but Lydia hardly heard them, not like she heard the murres—she wondered if the women of Fort Ross were instead accustomed to the sea bird's caws and haunted by screaming seals.

"This one!" Amos said. "It brings out your eyes. Try it."

She put it on.

"Are you happy?" he said.

"It's perfect," she said.

Exchanging a few more gruff words, Amos paid the trader. The couple walked back along the dock where crates of food and goods had been unloaded into a makeshift market and selected all of their usual provisions. Lydia watched on as Amos inspected several pallets of murre eggs a final time to send back with them.

Birds roved overhead, their droppings staining her new coat which lay heavy on her shoulders. Egging on the theatrics, the murre shrieked in hysterics at the sight of it, in spite of it all.

Born and raised in Northern California, **SOPHIA ZAKLIKOWSKI** *is a short story writer, essayist, and aspiring novelist. She was selected as a finalist for the Gold Line Press Fiction Chapbook Contest, and her writing has appeared in* Matchbox Magazine *and* LitHub. *Most recently, she presented her paper "Forest Fires & State Martyrs" at the University of Florida. She graduated from UC Santa Cruz, where she was awarded the Literature Department Best Creative Writing*

Senior Project Prize, and is now an MFA candidate and Poe/ Faulkner fellow at the University of Virginia in Charlottesville where she is working on her first novel. Current obsessions include: illuminated manuscripts; Borges, Bachmann, Dillard, and Duras; Appalachian music; tar pits and peat bogs; skin.

Funny Not Funny

Jenna Abrams

It's on 95, when the traffic frees up, when they're gliding in the sleet past the brown, newly gutting Delaware River, that Beth really starts to feel it: the difference in the drive, now that Eli is dead. The steering wheel flakes into her grinding fingers. Instead of her brother in the car, chain smoking in the passenger seat, cranking the volume, giving her shit about being away at college, it's this dude Deedee, a bassist she barely knows but has reluctantly agreed to drive, and to make things extra weird, he's sitting in the back, because apparently riding shotgun makes him nauseous. In the rearview, she watches his fingers twitching on invisible strings, head bobbing, his upside-down cross earring wobbling as they motor over the potholes and north, out of Philadelphia.

It has been thirty-six days since Eli jumped, slipped, dove, maybe some other fucking verb, some other explanation she'll never get in her life, into the Delaware River from the banks near Graffiti Pier. Thirty-four days since she took the flier for the last show he was booked to play from his wall at Hope House. Since then, it's been growing hot and insistent in her pocket, an unfulfilled promise that will combust if she doesn't honor it.

She's made this drive many times, Philly to the Borscht Belt for underground shows—Eli the unpredictable performer; Beth the reliable transportation. Metal shows, thrash throws, sludge and doom, all the words inhabiting the music Eli loved, held in empty spaces built for more polished guests. A hundred miles north of New York City, abandoned buildings dotted Sullivan County: empty hotels and rotting inns and camps, long forgotten on overgrown roads and at the edges of rebuilt towns. Their father told stories of earlier, more lively summers, but Beth has only ever known it as a land of empty, broken buildings, a place where the past lives right up on the surface with the present, instead of buried in the ground.

* * *

At the turnpike she digs for change and comes up short, swearing. Deedee leans forward, smelling like sweat and bike grease and tragically burned coffee, and explains how his anti-nausea meds make him feel.

"Not loopy," he says, "just empty. Like a black hole, okay, in the pit of your stomach. A singularity composed of the absence of nausea. A miracle." He hands her a quarter. Beth laughs, despite herself. He's wearing geriatric sunglasses obscuring half his pasty face (because fuck the weather, right?) and a huge black trench coat over a black denim vest. His wild hair and untrimmed beard; the dead, off-center front tooth, black, he'd said, from a kick to the mouth in a stage dive years ago; the way the space between that fucked tooth and the rest of them gaped like a sinister portal—if you didn't have context, you'd probably run. But there's a warmth in Deedee's chaos that translates to charisma. She recognizes it easily.

Just south of Newark, they gas up and ditch the highway, winding through North Jersey towards the New York border. Scott, frontman for the band Deedee will be playing bass in, has offered a spot to crash—his grandparents' old place on a neglected piece of land outside Cataspark. Deedee cranks the back window down and thumbs his lighter. Soon his cheeks are caving in on the cigarette. He stretches through the seats for the tape deck. A huge, thundering bass note sucker punches Beth's chest—one of Eli's tapes. She hits the eject button so hard it startles them both.

"No," she says, meaning to explain, but she doesn't have anything else.

Deedee switches to the radio. "What station is this?" he asks. "The programmed numbers."

"I don't know," she says. "Can you let it be? I'm doing you a favor."

"You don't know what radio station you listen to?"

"Whatever the main station is. You know, 80s, 90s, and today."

"Are you serious? 80s, 90s, and today? That's how you classify what you listen to?"

"I mean, sometimes," she says. "I like the variety. And the innocuousness. You don't ever listen to mainstream radio? I didn't invent the classification." She steals a look at Deedee. He's reaching for the volume knob.

"Oh, great." He jerks his head. "A funk station. This, I can work with."

Eli always controlled the music on these drives. Their first trip up here alone, her permit was barely in her hand. Just after they left the city behind, he rifled through his backpack and popped in a tape. A thick, rumbling note crept through the speakers. He curled his fingers in the air, clutching something she couldn't see.

"Do you hear that?" he asked. She swore his body was vibrating. Another note thrummed, identical. He punched her knee. "Do you feel it?"

He did a version of the same thing with his body every time, riffing off the first: squint, lean in acting like he couldn't reach the volume knob, hold out his hand to stop her from moving even if she was still. Listen to that build. Listen to it. Listen, listen—he was obsessed, could give the same speech a million times and never lose steam. She could barely keep up with him, so often it was easy to forget she was the older one.

*   *   *

Past Mahwah and into New York, everything gets emptier; frozen fields and vacant state parks, slate roads same as the sky. The funk station slides into fuzz and she turns it down. Deedee lowers his window, spits, and rolls it back up.

"I appreciate the ride," he says. "I keep meaning to get a license, but I never leave the city except for tours or shows, and there always seems to be somebody to take me."

"Must be nice."

"I should probably become more self-sufficient. Graduating to the real world again."

"What do you mean?"

"I only have a month to go in my program. Then I'm on my own." She'd picked him up at an adult partial support house, similar, as far as she could tell, to Hope House's adult programs, where Eli would've likely ended up if he'd made it to full-blown adulthood.

She almost says something about Hope House, but that would mean explaining Eli—worse, herself. Instead she asks, "What are you going to do?"

"I've thought a lot about this. Ready? Year one, I just stay inside listening to the Cure, overanalyzing my existence. Year two, I pull it together. Job-town, here I come. Decorate my cubicle and research Eagles stats so I have stuff to say to my coworkers, because I really just want to talk about '77 punk and the aftermath of Clinton's America. I'll marry my much smarter colleague because she thinks I'm mysterious, except it's only that I can't relinquish my illusion of coolness for fear of revealing my horrifying void. Her name is Maeve." He grins.

"The fuck, Deedee."

"Honestly, I don't know what I'm going to do, but I bet I'm going to have to learn to make new friends."

"What about Scott? Aren't you friends?"

"That's different. Scott is unfazed by my off-putting personality to a degree that should concern him. I mean regular people. I can't deal with the whole friend courting thing. I want to skip it. I want to immediately make spring rolls and watch Cronenberg movies in our socks. That weirds people out. But it's not weird, right? To want to immediately have a friend." He catches her eye in the mirror and nods, like they share a point of view of which she is unaware.

Eli made friends everywhere, though the depth of those friendships Beth could never be sure of—they existed in such a performative space, and Eli rarely spent quiet time with anyone alone. On the other hand, every interaction Beth had ever had was shrouded in wariness. Who knew why she was like this; she'd always been that way.

Deedee spends the next twenty minutes talking about what qualities make a movie "Cronenesque." At a light, she sees amidst the talking he is busily sewing a patch to his vest with tiny, tight stitches. Seamlessly, like the Cronenberg lecture never happened, he catches her eye in the mirror again and says, "But what I think about friends is that it doesn't take a lot for me to decide I like somebody, if the right combination of factors exist. If I like you, I like you."

"What kind of factors?"

"Hm," he tugs the thread, "well, I worshipped this bartender at my second-favorite bar, back when I used to hang out in bars all day. I knew three things about her and it was enough."

"What three things?"

"She listened to Iggy Pop, rode a Segway, and hated all poetry, inexplicably and on principle. She also said she thought of me as her 'strange little friend,' clearly demonstrating the hopelessness of a romantic relationship. So, I was definitely in love with her. Per my own criteria."

Beth rolls her eyes. "I don't think I get you."

"I get that a lot."

"You're funny, I guess." It doesn't feel like the right word. They pass a graffitied, decaying ice cream shop, roof collapsed in the middle. Their speed blurs its edges, blending it into the surroundings and out of time.

"Look," Deedee is saying, "maybe what I mean is, things that feel right are inexplicable sometimes. I was in love once for real, no joke. This woman Embla. She was this badass drummer from Iceland. She was smart as shit and unpredictable, and also very tender, and she would yell at me during sex. I would be on top of her and she would be yelling, telling me I wasn't doing a good job."

"That sounds terrible."

"No, no, it was amazing." Deedee leans wistfully against the window. His breath makes a wet circle in the glass. "It was a real connection. That's what I'm saying. That did it for me, and who cares why? I fucking loved it. I loved her. It was real."

*   *   *

After a stretch of nothing but pines and gutted buildings, there is Scott waving at the end of a long, frozen driveway. He hops in, asking how she's been in a tone that's full-on parental. Scott is older by a couple years, but of course he acts like it's a decade. He's got a big white patch on his coat featuring a zombie, *brains not bombs* lettered under its gaping mouth. He's a West Philly punk, so his whole thing is different from punks and metalheads in South Philly. Eli had embodied the latter perfectly, in ways Beth found anthropologically fascinating compared to guys like Scott. All the West Philly punks she knew had a cause; for Eli, "cause" was pretty vague. Eli was angry, but he was never going to identify what about. Scott would write a fucking manifesto if given a chance. Her impression of Scott was that he measured self-worth by articulation: how succinctly he could express his ethical or philosophical reasonings for whatever. But for Eli, it was about rage: how crazy he got in the pit, how much he didn't give a fuck if beer spilled on him, how loud he could yell. Eli didn't care about community building and DIY zines, Eli cared about breaking stuff. But in a way, it was the same—West, South, Jersey, whatever, always partially, crucially, performance. But that was everything, wasn't it? Eli would indulge these criticisms. But he'd find himself exempt.

Without him, her own malleability's contrast to a scene of people adhering fiercely to a particular identity is striking, too stark and chasmic to look at. Inside, as Deedee and Scott debate an album she's never heard of, she confirms her self-concept has been so knotted up with Eli's it's unclear what it is now. She's always teetered on the edge of his world, uncertain. It was exhausting, wanting to melt into it but also feeling drained: by the riffing on disloyal bassists or underrated sludge albums or which anarchist band wasn't really anarchist, the feeling she wasn't real without a bank of esoteric information. At Eli's shows she analyzed herself into panic, even as the music did wild, acutely joyful things to her brain. Okay, she loved it. And?

She hated going to his shows without a buffer. One of Eli's crusty, revolving former bandmates, usually. A hard-looking dude, any hard-looking dude to put her mind at ease. Either you looked the part or you brought someone who did. Hanging on Eli's periphery, she'd learned image mattered less if you had a dick. At shows, girls in mall clothes were side-eyed. Wear a polo as a guy, and you're just an ironic skinhead punk; dress plainly, in neutral clothes, and you're so authentic, you don't bother with aesthetics. But put that paper doll on a woman and the room looks at you like you're a fucking cop. Goddamnit. She hates everyone.

* * *

She says some of this later when they're in the backyard trying to get a fire lit, when the album debate has ended and she can get a fucking word in. The clouds have faded and it's brighter but freezing. Deedee crouches, working, as she and Scott pass a flask back and forth and shield him from the wind.

"Don't tell me you guys don't know what I'm talking about," she says, shivering.

"Okay," Scott says. "I hear you, but isn't that a little exaggerated? I see girls in the pit all the time. My house has hosted a bunch of girl-fronted bands. I mean, girls are legit, and punk has a long history of railing against exclusion. You think if you go to a show dressed in street clothes it makes a difference?" Then, perhaps sheepishly, "No offense."

"Dude," Deedee says, looking up. "'*Girls are legit?*'" Beth snorts, louder than she means to. She swallows a hit from the flask. The whiskey is bad but feels good going down. Scott does this thing with his gloved hand on his chin that makes it clear he's thinking carefully.

"Okay," he concedes, "that was dumb. But I'm just saying"— Scott is always *just saying* one thing or another—"if that was all girls' experience, they wouldn't be at shows. Most shows I've played had a mixed turnout."

"That doesn't mean shit. You truly think this scene is exempt from sexism and, like, 'coolness' politics?" She offers the flask to Deedee, who shakes his head.

"Okay but Beth, come on, in general punk is an inclusive space," Scott offers, like this actually means something. She rolls her eyes—but at what, exactly? Like she can judge it. Without Eli, who would probably give her righteous shit for debating Scott in the first place, she's more untethered than before.

*   *   *

The snow magnifies the sun's rays, bouncing light into glitter off the expanse of white that stretches into the trees. She's restless. Scott wants to stay by the fire, spitting high and crackly, but when she says she'd rather explore until they leave for the show, Deedee offers to join. Scott, content in his role as the dad, salutes, yelling to be careful, but not too careful.

They crush through the expanse of snow, past the husk of an ancient, decomposing tractor. The snow is deep and undisturbed, not even animal tracks dotting its surface. It makes her quiet; how untouched it all is, how easy it is to imagine all that the snow might cover. Deedee sniffs and spits as he walks. A many-colored cyclone patch on the shoulder of his trench catches her eye. It's the aesthetic Eli liked: chaotic. She hurries to him and taps it.

"Oh," Deedee says, twisting. "Obscure 80s psychedelic band. I found it at this shop on South Street. Kind of a weirdo, who runs it. It's next to a vegan hot dog shop now."

"Fuck South Street." She cringes. "It's a fucking tourist trap." Eli had felt that way, and she'd adopted it, and now she agreed, so the difference didn't matter. But Deedee is grinning.

"Okay, great. I disagree. I mean—yes, it's a tourist trap. But the roots! You can't call yourself a Philadelphian and hate South Street. It's like New Yorkers who hate Times Square." For effect, perhaps, he's stopped. Overhead, a bird calls from the stripped trees. In these same woods, east maybe, there is a pond she and Eli discovered as kids, hidden on an overgrown path that crested over an enormous hill before dropping into a rich, dense grove of red maples. She wonders if she could find it now without him.

"I hate Times Square," she says.

"Fuck you!" Deedee laughs. "I love Times Square. You can't pretend it doesn't exist. It's the apex of American civilization! You can do anything in Times Square. You can buy porn. You can buy a stuffed animal so big you have to enlist strangers to help carry it home. You can go from McDonald's to McDonald's drinking coffee and peeing." She's most often seen Eli argue like this—no real acid, like he finds joy in disagreement.

"What does that have to do with South Street?"

"It's a piece of the city's history, man! You don't see the value of immortalizing a city with junk? Shot glasses with cartoon dudes puking out cheesesteaks that say *Illadelphia*? Merchandising the place memorialized by the opening line to the iconic Fear song 'I Don't Care About You?' The place Boyz II Men's 'Motownphilly' video was filmed?"

Deedee takes a breath. He's looking at the sky now. "It's mythologizing serious and silly points of identity. It's self-referential. It's nostalgia, which I'm a sucker for. It means my city has an identity that can be, okay, flattened and commodified, but also immortalized. I love that. Am I overthinking it? My therapist says if anything is the end of me it'll be a train of my own thoughts running me over until I die."

Beth looks at him. He is too much, too recognizable, or not at all recognizable, maybe that's it, his wide-open self too bright. He hurts her eyes. "I'm cold," she says. "Let's keep going. There used to be a clubhouse and dining hall this way, part of a camp." Deedee falls in. After a minute, she says, "Your therapist did not tell you a train of your thoughts would run you over until you died."

"Okay," Deedee concedes. "Technically, those were my words. She repeated them afterwards, slowly, the way you do when you're horrified at what someone has just said."

"And then?" Beth turns back. She can't tell, in the light, what his face is doing.

"Back off, cop." He flashes her his dead tooth. "Isn't that protected information?"

*   *   *

They're almost to the hill where the clubhouse sits, at least she thinks. Winter makes everything blurry and unrecognizable. She closes her eyes, trying to find a word for what the world smells like covered in snow. When she opens them, Deedee has run ahead, bellowing as his boots puncture the crust before he disappears through the trees. She follows, placing her feet in the spaces he has broken open. At the edge of the woods, she sees his silhouette against the sky, halfway up the hill already. By the time she catches up, he's at the clubhouse basement door, hanging just broken enough from its hinges.

The basement is very dark. Deedee, apparently the kind of person who carried a pocket knife as a kid, pulls a slender flashlight from his pocket. The beam catches a room filled with junk: saw blades, broken tools, rotted construction paper. Beth sifts through a damp pile of children's books on a table. On the first floor of this place, years ago, she and Eli took some ugly coffee mugs to destroy and record the sound for one of his tapes. She liked smashing them against the bulkhead doors at their uncle's place, leaving shards everywhere.

Deedee points the flashlight at an inky corner and jumps back, swearing. She sucks in her breath. Three figures—mannequins, her brain registers, and she calms down—sit in a circle, dressed in green t-shirts with white outlines of pine trees on them.

"Well, disturbing," Deedee says, but he's already squatting beside them, laughing. He lifts a rusted saw blade and hands her the flashlight. "So, they come to life and kill us with this, right?" She looks to the slim rectangle of light from the cracked door, shifting in the wind, then back at the mannequins. Their eyes seem to be everywhere and nowhere at once. They are faded and simplified, only the suggestion of a face, the bland beige of the eyes the same color as the nose the same as the cheeks, all of it the same. If she stares at one long enough to blur her vision, she can't be sure she is looking at a face at all, and if she lets it blur even more, the featureless smear begins to remind her of herself.

Deedee pulls a tin from his vest. "Shine here." He dumps weed into a paper and extracts a pinch of tobacco from a cigarette. She sits close while he rolls, clutching the flashlight. When he's finished he hands her the spliff. "You know the show space for tonight?" he asks. "It's an old hotel. A rare fully sanctioned show." He kisses his fingers. "Maintained by some biker from Long Island who wound up buying it like a decade ago. '92 maybe?"

"Yeah, I've been there before. I've seen that guy. He has a weird name. Teeth?"

"Tooth!" Deedee laughs. "Fuck if I know why. He has more than one. He only comes up for Motörhead cover bands. It's the dude's brand. Respect."

She rubs her hands on her jeans and flicks the lighter. "My brother's band had kind of a big following before he died. They played a lot around here." She names Eli's last band and sucks in a big hit. Deedee raises his eyebrows in recognition.

"Really? I knew that band, man. I remember him. I didn't know—I mean, Scott mentioned your brother had passed recently." He makes a little motion with his head and his hands. She holds a sound tight in her throat. "He said any more wasn't his to share. Honestly, he told me so I wouldn't step in it unintentionally, with a poorly timed joke. I didn't know that was who he meant." He grimaces. "I'm very sorry. What happened to him?"

What happened: that empty space had such incredible power, a singularity of uncertainty she knew would swallow her whole if she let it. The fucked part was, almost any explanation was believable, which meant nothing stood clear as an answer. Eli could have slipped, hit his head, could have been acting on a dare, could have been so fucked out of his mind he didn't know what he was doing.

Or he could have killed himself, that too. Their parents accept the explanation of an accident, but it doesn't do anything for her. In the end, the only knowable thing is Eli is dead. It's not him who has to live in the after.

"He went into the Delaware River." She passes Deedee the glowing spliff. "Just went into the Delaware, and didn't come out."

She was fifteen when she started going with Eli to the shows he was playing in the city. At twelve he was often the youngest there; she one of the only girls. She'd find him after, when he was wild-eyed and slimed in sweat, ranting urgently. Trying to explain what it did for him. At a diner once, late, when he was in eighth grade, one of the nights she took him out after a show for a grilled cheese and sat with him until he was sober and calm enough to go home, he pleaded with her. He had a string of cheese stuck to his chin. "Inside me," he said, "there is a scream, louder than any sound you've ever heard, and quieting that scream is my entire life and I'm exhausted, do you understand?"

"I'm trying," she said, sucking up the dregs of her milkshake with a loud hollow sound. She looked at her brother's eye, swelling a darkening blue from some hit he'd taken gladly.

After a couple local shows, she stopped waiting by the door. She grew bolder when Eli performed. She thrashed through crowds, shedding herself until she was transformed into a monster in the pit, possessed by a force she hoped belonged to her and also felt stolen off her brother. She cracked her chin, took elbows to the face, contorted her body to dense, indulgent riffs, roared when a build crescendoed and dove into a gravid, lurching drop. She was inflamed with the feeling—frightening, magnetic—of giving herself over to something louder than her own head. So, she did understand what had happened to him, in a sense. The world Eli lived in was an excellent place to hide. Everyone is fucked up, rattling, howling, expressing—so you can't tell the difference between the performative scream and the one that needs to be listened to. You hear it all the same, until you don't.

In the basement Deedee passes the spliff back. "He was at Hope House," Beth says, inhaling. "You know it? In the youth program. He was about to age out."

"You're kidding." He's quiet. "I would've hated that place as a teenager. Um. What was he like?" Deedee's pauses are surprising, cadent, so strange she must talk to fill them. But any story flattens, captures only one angle. She wants to start from the beginning, but she was only three, so she doesn't remember Eli being born. She often pretended they were twins, his existence felt so tied to her own. If she starts from their collective beginning: the first time she tried to hold her brother, he wound up his tiny fist and punched her in the face.

It's easier to talk to the mannequins than Deedee. "We came up here as kids," she tells them. "My uncle Sol owned a small inn with my dad. It closed the year I was born but we'd come stay in the property every summer, until they stopped speaking. But before, Eli and I spent every day together—I was kind of in charge of him. At home, too. Our parents weren't prepared for him, and they stopped trying early. Up here, as long as we were at our uncle's to eat and sleep, they didn't care. They liked me to keep him distracted, away."

She inches closer to Deedee and the mannequins. If it had been Eli who discovered them, he'd have found a way for it to mean something. But they're so blank, and more than anything now, that frightens her. She hits the spliff again and passes it, her tongue unwieldy, fabricky.

"One time up here, we discovered this hidden pond. It became our place. You had to get over this huge hill to find the path, so tall you can't tell if there's anything after it. Eli loved it. He had this way of talking about hearing a song for the first time, how it was like the way that hill cut off into the treeline. You can't see beyond, can't tell if everything in the world drops off a cliff or not. That's how he felt about the first listen, to a doom song or sludge or whatever."

"The build to an apex," Deedee nods. "The other side is a question."

"You have to trust that something is there. He said that's the future unknown, the good kind of unknown."

"What's the bad kind of unknown?"

She presses her chin to her knees. "Past is the bad kind." They are a tight circle now, the five of them. The three inches of light from the cracked door and the pale wash of the flashlight, propped against a mannequin knee, catch everyone's faces except hers. Like she's on an unlit stage alone, facing an illuminated suggestion of an audience. "We went back all the time. When we were older and there were shows up here, he liked to go before performing. We'd ride over that hill to the water, leave our bikes on the rocks. You have to push through a huge tangle of lily pads to get to the middle, where it's very deep, much deeper than you'd think, and the water is so cool and so dark, not just in color but in weight, depth. When Eli was in that pond all his rage just kind of dissolved. We never dove to the bottom. I think the uncertainty of how deep it went and what was down there scared us. It's the only thing my brother was ever truly afraid of."

"Is it here?" Deedee asks.

"It's around here. The snow makes it hard to tell."

He nods. "Tell me something else."

"There was one time, after a storm, years after we'd found it. He'd eaten all this acid. He sailed up the hill like magic, and it was so slick, I couldn't keep up, and I was sure one of us would crash. I'd never seen anyone on acid before. He was rambling about leaves and how many there were and how the roots went all the way into the earth and didn't I wish I had roots like that? When I got to the pond, he'd turned his bike upside down and was doing a handstand, balanced on the tires, and he fell. When he stood, there was this big stream of blood running over his eye and I couldn't, like, see him in his own face, you know? Then he grabbed my bike, threw it into the pond, and came at me swinging, making these wild sounds. I jumped in and swam to the middle. He came after me, shouting—he was shouting, *To live is to suffer! To live is to suffer!* I didn't know what he was talking about, until I went to college a year later, and took a fucking Intro to Philosophy class. He would appreciate that. This fifteen-year-old, quoting Nietzsche on acid, to a void of understanding. I mean, it's funny, right? He would think it was funny. It's also not, I guess. Because we were both suffering, or something."

"It's both," Deedee says. "When I do the grocery shopping for my program, I put the eggs next to the chicken in the refrigerator because I think it's funny." He blows on his hands. "But it's also not funny. Because, you know, it's all dead." The hands go back into his pockets.

"Thanks, Deedee."

"I'm sorry. Please don't stop."

"Well, he started sobbing, so I swam to him and held him while he tried to fight me. When he calmed down I turned him onto his back and we floated forever, until way after dark, and before we climbed out, he gave me this funny, awkward hug in the water that almost sunk us, and told me he was glad I was there and that he would never leave me." She says the last part like it's all one word. It feels like a long time before Deedee makes any noise. The spliff has gone out but he tilts his head and relights it.

"I saw him onstage a few times," he says finally. "I was at that show two years ago in Hollow Falls, when he smashed the light. You see that?"

During the last song, Eli had yanked a lightbulb from a broken lamp, smashed it into his chest, and spat the glass into the crowd. Everyone had gone wild over it. Because fuck the risk, right? All that mattered was the intensity. She could almost taste what it would feel like, to not fear anything like him. To fear neither mediocrity nor death. Later, he hugged her, and when she caught her reflection in the warped, metallic bathroom mirror, she saw his blood smeared across her face, and inside, in a growing place, she liked it.

"I didn't know him," Deedee is saying, "but I think there are some people you can tell a lot about by how they perform, you know? And your brother, he was so fucking present, every time I saw that band play. He was so in it, like he was trying to work something out every moment he was up there. Maybe that's why he did shit like that—he was trying to push through to something else. You know?"

"Maybe," she says. "I wish I knew what it was."

*   *   *

As they pass the spliff back and forth Deedee starts talking about how long he's lived in the city and how it took a decade to build his reputation, so he can never move, because how could he ever start over in another place? She hears the words but they don't make sense.

"What's that like, for that to matter so much?" she asks. Deedee laughs.

"It's stupid," he says, "but I choose for it to be important, because something has to be." She puts her hand on his shoulder and tries to zip her coat. Under his trench she can see the patch he sewed to his vest in the car, adhered with deliberate, even stitches; so careful, so unlike the rest of him. She asks about the band. Deedee holds out his hands, palms up, his fingers curled inward, like he's clutching something invisible.

"They're so good," he starts, and then, "so dark," like it's the same thing. "Ultimate doom, crushing." But she asks him to explain it to her without the lingo.

"Just, what does it do for you?" she asks. "What does it feel like?" The joy this elicits on Deedee's face is enough to balance every moment she's spent bewildered by him.

"Okay," he says. "So, imagine it's the apocalypse. The world has ended. And you're maybe the only person left in the world. And you're riding a motorcycle through the desert." He nods heavily, the damp crutch of the dead spliff limp between his lips. His fists are raised in front of him, gripping an invisible motorcycle. "That's what it sounds like. That's what it feels like."

"Where do you get a motorcycle after the apocalypse?" she asks.

He's shaking his head. "No, no. Just be there. The world has descended into chaos, you're alone, you've fucking *survived*, okay? And you're riding a motorcycle through the desert. That's what it feels like."

"But what happens after?" she asks. "After the apocalypse, after the motorcycle in the desert? What does that sound like? Please— what can I listen to that sounds like that?" She doesn't mean to sound so desperate. Deedee is as hushed as she's seen him, making her wildly self-conscious, examining what she's said for the weight his silence has given it. Her head is so, so heavy. Deedee reaches for her abandoned jacket zipper.

"Here," he says, tugging. "Let me help."

*   *   *

She feels horrible but also calm, empty, like she's poured out the light tube and the bikes and the diner and the tapes and Eli's floating form, and the way he clutched her infantly as she held him, the weight of the pond and his whisper, a promise severely broken, expelled it all into the room and is now floating above herself, watching. Deedee's talking sounds like music; no words, only the boom of his voice and how it chugs forward. When she refocuses he's talking about burning crop fields and she asks if he can talk about himself without using metaphors.

"What's the point?" he asks. She doesn't have an answer; it's the kind of question Eli asked all the time. Instead, surprising them both, she leans over and kisses him. He hesitates, but he kisses her back. The kiss has this practiced feel—the motions, but also the fluidity and emotion behind it. Like he knows what he should do, but also what he should feel, like he's performing a feeling for the sake of them both. She pulls herself into his lap and he reaches up to touch her face. Then, she has to pull away because she realizes she doesn't really want him, what she wants is to force her tongue down his throat until his jaw unhinges, until it breaks, cracks open, until he becomes a snake, more; she wants to hurt him, hurt both of them. When she gets off his lap she is sobbing hard and her hair is caught in a button on his collar and while she untangles it neither of them says anything.

When she is calm, Deedee stands. "Listen," he says, and his voice is more grounded, adult. "I don't think that kiss needs to mean anything. But you are my friend, my real friend. Cronenberg-in-socks kind of friend. I want you to know." She wipes her face and puts out a hand so Deedee can pull her up. She lifts one of the mannequins, cradling it in her armpit.

"We're taking this." She doesn't look at him, but she can feel the yes.

*   *   *

The show is in the husk of an inn off a dirt mountain road. Beth carries the mannequin on one shoulder. The guy at the door takes their five dollars and waves them in, his inexplicably bare arms covered in bad stick-and-poke tattoos, half the ink fallen out. Inside, Scott finds the sound manager, engaging her with dramatic gestures by the stage, which is built on the remnants of a concierge desk. Beth hands the mannequin to Deedee, who promises to incorporate it somehow. Everyone is wandering, or planted near the bar: a door across two stools, flanked by coolers and plastic cups. A girl with velvety green hair holds a bottle in the air. A destroyed couch sits askew in a corner. During a show Eli played here last year, a crowd drunk on his performance shoved metal chairs into the wall, legs-first. Now they hang there, sideways and weird and useless.

She can still hear it easily—that first song, on that first drive. Initially almost noteless, a vibration from every direction, a hum in the back of a throat. As the first note faded, the second dropped in, and the third, and the guitar moved behind her chest somehow, dragging her to the apex. Then the guitar shrieked upwards, and the drums joined with thick, sinewy, doomy beats, then the bass, everything crushing together. It was loud—LOUD, that moment when it all came in, the world suddenly yanked forward. Like being able to feel a sound and hear a feeling all at once; the lurch under her ribs when the build dropped off and cascaded into the first rolling, thumping, exquisite riff, moving with certainty toward the uncertain next.

Most of the crowd is gathered near the stage as Scott's band finishes sound check. She pushes to the front. Deedee steps over and whispers in Scott's ear. It's a long whisper, involved, Scott nodding vigorously, followed by some shuffling. Scott mouths something to the sound manager, who returns a thumbs up as

Scott steps back. Deedee stands at the front instead. He pulls the mic from the stand with a screech amidst cheers of recognition.

"Hey, you motherfuckers! Thanks, thanks. I'm filling in for these folks tonight—Gia broke her hand, obviously an obstacle for a bassist. Scott has graciously agreed to let me take the lead on this first one. We're gonna improvise a song up here, and hopefully you'll let us live." He makes a little bow to Scott, who throws him devil horns with his free hand. Deedee grins, his fucked-up tooth swallowing light, and squats to put his arm around the mannequin, which he has seated on the stage. Then he stands, mashing his teeth against the mic again. "Hell yeah. This new song is for a friend of ours!" he shouts. "It's about what happens after the apocalypse." He reaches out, the mic in his hand, and points it right at her. Then he strikes his bass.

The first notes grip, indescribably low and heavy. Deedee's vocals start quiet, slowly transforming into a roar. At its core, it's doom, or psychedelic? It's more, beyond, Deedee's voice oscillating between gravelly moans and a high wailing that's almost beautiful, operatic, as the music increases in weight, getting louder in a way that isn't only about volume. She pushes her vibrating body into the pit; notes snarling, epically loud, impossible and distorted, buzzed out of perceivable form; onstage Deedee is howling into the mic on his knees, he's crawling on the floor, he's tossing the mannequin into the crowd, he's writhing on his back with the mic cord wrapped around him. She watches the mannequin surf across the sea of hands before she takes the shoulder of the dude next to her and follows it up, up, until she's floating on the crowd as the unraveling riff explodes, an engine roaring under her and a desert stretching in front of her and the sand moving with the bass and her heart pounding with all of it, carried on by a magnified, unstoppable wave of sound, rocking her back and forth and forward through the sludge.

JENNA ABRAMS *was born in Massachusetts. Her work has been published in* Epoch *and is forthcoming in*

Driftwood *(2023). Her work has also been selected as a finalist for the* Florida Review *2021-2022 Jeanne Leiby Memorial Chapbook Award, the* Quarterly West *2021 Chapbook Contest, the* Yemassee *2021 Chapbook Contest, and the* Indiana Review *2021 Fiction Prize, and shortlisted for the* Masters Review *Anthology IX. She earned an MFA at the University of California - Irvine, and has received support from the Community of Writers, Vermont Studio Center, and the Elizabeth George Foundation. She lives in Los Angeles. Twitter: @ner_ves*

CPSIA information can be obtained
at www.ICGtesting.com
Printed in the USA
BVHW050006280623
666449BV00016B/901